MONTANA ★ MAVERICKS

Welcome to Montana—the home of bold men
and daring women, where more than fifty tales
of passion, adventure and intrigue unfold
beneath the Big Sky. Don't miss a single one!

AVAILABLE FEBRUARY 2009

AVAILABLE APRIL 2009

AVAILABLE MAY 2009

Montana ★ MAVERICKS™

JENNIFER MIKELS

Rich, Rugged... Ruthless

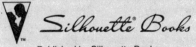
Silhouette Books

Published by Silhouette Books
America's Publisher of Contemporary Romance

If you purchased this book without a cover you should be aware
that this book is stolen property. It was reported as "unsold and
destroyed" to the publisher, and neither the author nor the
publisher has received any payment for this "stripped book."

Special thanks and acknowledgment to Jennifer Mikels
for her contribution to the Montana Mavericks series.

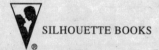 SILHOUETTE BOOKS
®

ISBN-13: 978-0-373-31051-7

RICH, RUGGED...RUTHLESS

Recycling programs
for this product may
not exist in your area.

Copyright © 2000 by Harlequin Books S.A.

All rights reserved. Except for use in any review, the reproduction
or utilization of this work in whole or in part in any form by any
electronic, mechanical or other means, now known or hereafter
invented, including xerography, photocopying and recording, or in
any information storage or retrieval system, is forbidden without
the written permission of the editorial office, Silhouette Books,
233 Broadway, New York, NY 10279 U.S.A.

This is a work of fiction. Names, characters, places and incidents are
either the product of the author's imagination or are used fictitiously,
and any resemblance to actual persons, living or dead, business establishments,
events or locales is entirely coincidental.

This edition published by arrangement with Harlequin Books S.A.

® and TM are trademarks of Harlequin Books S.A., used under license.
Trademarks indicated with ® are registered in the United States Patent
and Trademark Office, the Canadian Trade Marks Office and in other
countries.

Visit Silhouette Books at www.eHarlequin.com

Printed in U.S.A.

JENNIFER MIKELS

is from Chicago, Illinois, but resides now in Phoenix, Arizona, with her husband, two sons and a shepherd-collie. She enjoys reading, sports, antiques, yard sales and long walks. Though she's done technical writing in public relations, she loves writing romances and happy endings.

Prologue

"A curse on you, Max Montgomery. You'll get yours one day."

Max leaned back in the forest-green wing chair behind his desk and watched Dwayne Melrose storm from the office. As president of Whitehorn Savings and Loan bank, Max could have let one of the loan officers handle Melrose, but because he'd once dated Melrose's daughter while in his teens, he'd given the man a personal appointment. What had been the point? He'd known the outcome before Dwayne had arrived.

Annoyed with himself for even considering an extension, Max pushed back from the highly polished cherry desk. It was past banking hours, too late, but tomorrow morning he'd authorize foreclosure on the Melrose ranch. He couldn't let Melrose's words touch him. The man had signed an agreement with Whitehorn Savings and Loan, and should uphold his part of it.

He knew people viewed him as hard-hearted in business, but he believed in studying financial statements, not listening to sob stories. The bank's success mattered more than his personal popularity.

Standing, he stuffed a statement of the quarterly budget into his briefcase and shut it. He viewed himself as pragmatic, perhaps demanding. He had lived the life of the indulged, of one who was used to people doing as he said. From the time he was a little boy, he'd had servants catering to his needs. That was a part of life as Ellis and Deidre Montgomery's son. As a child he'd had the finest schooling, and as a man, he'd worked hard for his own success.

With a glance at the digital clock on his desk, he grimaced. He was going to arrive late for his father's political speech to a ranchers group in Bozeman. Ellis expected him to come. Rachel, too, had probably received barked orders to make an appearance. Having his grown children in attendance presented the right image. Ellis wanted to be governor so badly he couldn't think about anything else.

Max stepped out of his office, nodded to Edna Redden, his personal assistant, stationed at her desk, but without a word he passed by. He knew she was widowed, had two married children and a grandson. By choice he knew nothing else about her. He kept his distance from her—from everyone.

Beneath a darkening sky, he climbed into his

gleaming, black BMW and headed down the town's main street. In passing, he noticed the Hip Hop was jammed. It was fried chicken night, a crowd pleaser. He'd gone a few times, sat alone at the counter and read the newspaper, but talked to no one. It made sense not to make friendships. As the bank's president, he held the purse strings to a lot of people's dreams.

Because he was running late, before reaching the edge of town, he decided to shortcut down an unpaved road that bisected the woods and cut twenty minutes from traveling time. Within half an hour, his car's headlights beamed on the dark road. He didn't need light to know exactly where he was. As if the car had a will of its own, he found himself slowing it at a certain curve. He stared at the woods and in the direction of the rocky embankment where his youngest sister had died.

During those last seconds, had Christina been afraid? Or had her last seconds passed without her being aware someone was behind her with a shovel raised over her head, that danger was near? He hoped for that. He hoped she hadn't been frightened.

Years ago when they'd been closer, he remembered how scared she'd been of a spider that had floated down from a barn rafter and nearly landed on her shoulder. How old had she been? Three. Maybe four, he recalled. He'd wrapped an arm around her shoulder until she'd stopped crying.

But he hadn't been with her on the last day of her life. In the weeks before her disappearance she'd telephoned him a few times—including the day before she died. He'd heard a break in her voice. Had she needed to cry that last day? Had she needed him?

Under his breath, he swore and jammed a foot on the accelerator, irritated he was dwelling on something he couldn't change. Why the overload of guilt this evening? Nothing could bring her back. Stupid. It was stupid to keep thinking about it. He eased his foot off the pedal. Speed wouldn't help, he reminded himself. He couldn't go fast enough to get away from his own thoughts.

Damn it, he should have been there for her, should have gone to her. *I'm sorry.* He wished he could say those words to her.

With the window cracked open, he could smell the pines that bordered one side of the road. A chill still clung to the evening air in late May. Instinctively Max braked at a curve, but not soon enough. He caught a glimpse of an outline. Its doe eyes glazed, the deer had frozen, trapped in the beam of the headlights.

Gripping the steering wheel, Max veered right and faced inky darkness. As the car bounced over the shoulder of the road and the uneven ground that edged the dark woods, the silhouette of a tree trunk appeared. He saw it only a second before the car slammed into it. The air bag inflated, but his head whacked against the side window, snapped back, then hit again. So did his arm. Something cracked. A bone.

Max groaned, tried to reach up and touch his head. Pain shot through his arm. Nausea rose. With the side of his head pressed to the window, dizzy, he started to close his eyes. The last thing he saw was the silhouette of the deer dashing into the woods.

One

Voices intruded on a dream. Max grappled to hold on to it, but it fluttered away and left him with the sounds, an annoyed masculine voice and a more worried, feminine one. Slowly he opened his eyes for the second time that morning. His head ached, as though someone had taken a hammer to it. He blinked, struggling for coherence. Through slitted eyes, he took in the room, painted a soft blue.

He was in a hospital, he remembered now. Earlier when he'd awakened, everything had been fuzzy. He'd learned then where he was. He'd been in an accident, the doctor had told him. Max remembered jerking on the steering wheel, seeing a tree looming, a deer running. But not much more. The panic he'd felt then returned now. He'd be damned if he could remember his name or how old he was. And who these people in his room were.

"Max?"

He focused on the woman, a pregnant woman, who was standing at the foot of the bed.

"Max, thank God." Pretty, with dark brown hair, she rushed to the side of the bed.

Who the hell was she? He turned his attention to the man. Tall, somewhat portly, he had raven-black hair. It was too black for a man his age. Max guessed he was in his late fifties and using something to cover his gray. His face was angular, his eyes blue.

"Max, we've been so worried about you," the woman said.

He looked down as she grabbed his hand. Was that his hand? It was large, strong-looking. The nails were trim and clean. It was the hand of a man who didn't do manual labor. He raised the hand and stared at it, turned it to examine the palm. The other arm was in a cast to below his wrist.

"We know everything is confusing, Max."

How did she know? He barely knew what was happening. The doctor had told him his name—Max Montgomery. He rolled it over in his mind. He could have gotten worse. Okay, so he knew who he was. But who was this woman? Wife, fiancée, cousin, sister, friend? He wanted to close his eyes.

"Max, don't close your eyes again," she practically pleaded.

He felt a gentle grip on his right forearm.

"Max, please." She shook his arm. "Please, stay awake."

Max opened his eyes because she sounded so anxious, so caring. "What's your name?" he asked, and swallowed hard against the dryness in his mouth. "Who are you? My wife?"

In a flash, hurt rushed into her dark blue eyes. "Rachel. I'm Rachel." She mustered up a smile. "I'm your sister. And you're not married."

"He knows that. Don't you, Max?" the man insisted, taking a place on the other side of the bed.

Now what? Another face? Another person he couldn't remember. "Who are you?"

Instead of hurt as he'd seen in the woman's face, the man's expression delivered a message of annoyance. "Damn. This is impossible. We can't have this. Rachel, we have to do something about this." He fixed another stare on Max. "I'm your father. I'm Ellis Montgomery."

He could have been saying, "I'm the man in the moon." Max didn't know him. He wasn't too sure he wanted to know him. "I'm tired." Anger and fear had him in their grasp and he wanted only to be alone. His mind was so empty. He'd tried to remember a day, a minute from his childhood, but nothing came to mind. Nothing. He swallowed down the pressure tightening his throat. He needed these people to go before he did something stupid, before he lost it. "Just leave me alone, damn it."

Standing by the nurses' station, Samantha Carter heard the raised, angry male voice. She knew it belonged to Max Montgomery. She'd hung out at the Medical/Surgical Unit, waiting to talk to the doctor of one of her patients and had listened to the gossip. Max Montgomery had regained consciousness after two days.

Rich. Handsome. Arrogant. Hard-as-nails and ruthless in business. Impossible. Those were the words people used to describe him. A few more could be added since his accident. He'd broken an arm, and while medication kept the pain at bay, he'd no doubt be ornery with the cast on his arm hindering his every movement.

If he was difficult now, she figured he had a right to be. She'd heard that he also had amnesia. That sometimes happened after head injuries. She assumed it was a temporary condition. Regardless, it wouldn't be easy for a proud, controlling man to ask for help.

Samantha noticed the sister scurrying from the room. Poor thing. Quite pregnant, she looked ready to burst into tears. Often the problems of illness proved just as difficult for family members as for the patient.

"He could be the town's most eligible bachelor," one of the nurses gushed. "So handsome."

Samantha agreed. She remembered seeing him at the bank. With chiseled good looks, raven-colored hair and broad shoulders, he had only to walk into a room for people to notice him. He held himself tall and strode with an air of arrogance as if he knew he was right—always.

But Samantha hadn't expected their paths to ever cross. He was Mayor Ellis Montgomery's only son.

She was Samantha Carter, Teresa Carter's love child. He'd attended the finest schools; she'd gone to the one across a field from the trailer court where she lived. Theirs were completely different life-styles.

Turning, she found herself the object of Shirley Cassidy's attention, though the head nurse was talking to Rachel Montgomery Henderson.

"She doesn't knuckle under easily?" Rachel asked.

"Not that one," Shirley assured her, and gestured in Samantha's direction.

Sam laughed and started toward them. "Are you talking about me?"

Shirley met her halfway. "I heard you're between jobs."

Sam had considered applying for a position as a physical therapist at Whitehorn Memorial. Therapeutic exercise and rehabilitation was her specialty, but if she could find something with a more flexible schedule, she would prefer it to the ten-hour hospital shift. "Did you hear about something?"

"Rachel Henderson is looking for a private nurse for her brother," she said, pointedly looking at Rachel, who was only feet away now. "I'll leave you two to talk."

"Thank you, Shirley." Rachel turned the smile on Samantha. "Shirley said you've lived here five years."

"Yes, I've been around. Sometimes I work in Big Timber or Billings." Sam wasn't certain Rachel had heard her, because as the town's mayor came out of his son's room, her attention shifted.

Known as an affable and loquacious man, he delivered a good morning to a nurse passing by. A politician above all else, he would present a public face no matter what was happening in his personal life. "Rachel," he called to her.

Rachel answered with a nod. "Be right there." Her gaze returned to Sam. "Perhaps I could meet you at the Hip Hop, and we could talk."

"Fine." Sam brushed back strands of her curly red hair. She had planned to leave the hospital in a few moments, anyway, to stop in at a former patient's house. "One o'clock, Mrs. Henderson?" she asked, to give herself time for her plans.

"Perfect. And please call me Rachel," she insisted.

As Rachel joined her father, Sam waited to say goodbye to Shirley.

She was nearby completing a conversation with Gavin Nighthawk. A good-looking Native American, the doctor turned the heads of several nurses as he strode to the elevator.

Slipping her purse strap over her shoulder, Sam waited another moment for Shirley to finish making a notation on a patient's chart, then waved and gave her a "See you." She headed to her car and made her way through town, her thoughts on her former patient.

Billy had needed extensive physical therapy after an accident had caused him to be tossed from the bed of a pickup. He had endured several operations and months of physical therapy. But at thirteen, Billy was unstoppable.

Within ten minutes Sam was braking at the curb in

front of his parents' house. Pleasure swept through her the moment she heard the thumping sound of a basket-ball. When she neared the house, she saw Billy outma-neuvering his brother to the net. Moments like this, when she witnessed a patient resuming his life, gave her the most joy in her work.

"Sam! Hi!" he yelled when he spotted her. "Come on and play."

Smiling, Sam crossed to him.

At five minutes to one and in good spirits after her visit with Billy, Sam entered the Hip Hop. Janie Austin, the café manager, waved before the door closed behind Sam. Janie, a slim woman, was in her twenties, married to Deputy Sheriff Reed Austin. Her blond ponytail swinging, the pretty manager hustled toward the cook's counter to place an order. Sam wandered past several tables before spotting Rachel Henderson in one of the booths.

"As I told you at the hospital, my brother needs a private nurse," Rachel said once Sam had ordered a cup of coffee. "You heard he has partial amnesia?"

There was love here between brother and sister, Sam decided. Although from all she'd heard about the town's bank president, he was as stingy with affection as he was with the bank's money. "Yes." Everyone was talking about Max's amnesia. They always talked about the Montgomerys. And someone with amnesia wasn't an everyday occurrence in Whitehorn.

"Fortunately he's intellectually the same. He was

always so bright," she said with pride. "I'm glad he didn't lose that. But he has lost so much more. He doesn't remember anything prior to the accident."

Sam offered encouraging words. "In cases like this, amnesia is usually short-termed."

"Yes, we've been told that. We were so scared for him after the accident." Worry laced Rachel's voice. "When we learned he was okay and he was out of danger, I—we expected him to be in a foul mood."

Sam felt for the woman. Clearly she loved her brother, but didn't know how to reach him. From what Sam had heard about Ellis Montgomery's indifference to his children, she assumed he wasn't much help. This woman with the kind eyes was on her own.

Rachel twisted the napkin in her hands. "With the head injury, he shouldn't be alone until he recovers his memory."

She had a major problem. Sam easily guessed what it was as she detected a hint of desperation in Rachel's voice. Because of her brother's reputation as difficult and demanding, she was worried she wouldn't find someone to take the job.

Rachel spoke words that almost verified Sam's thought. "Quite honestly, he's not an easy man. He's distant. Solitary."

Sam could have told her no explanation was necessary. She'd heard the talk about him. "What man is easy?"

"Like I said, he's not." Affection blended with the amusement in Rachel's tone. "But he's a lovable pain."

Sam wished she could reassure her, could tell her

that she understood men. Thanks to her mother, plenty of them had wandered through her life. One thing she'd learned early was that a man didn't handle illness well. She had no doubt that Max Montgomery wouldn't be any different.

"His housekeeper quit the day before he had his accident, and…and the cook left a few weeks before that. I don't know why. But that means you'd have to cook, too." Rachel rushed the words. "I promise I'll try to get someone hired as quickly as possible." Momentarily distracted, Rachel's gaze suddenly shifted toward a nearby booth, to the fortyish, rather slender woman with graying blond hair. "Hello, Kate."

Judge Kate Randall Walker smiled back. "Hi."

"Has father talked you into running on the ticket with him?"

Faint lines crinkled at the corners of the judge's eyes with her smile. "I'm not interested in a political career or being attorney general. How is your brother?"

"He's doing better."

"What he needs is a good woman to sweeten up his sour disposition. But what woman in town is bold enough to try?"

Rachel may have laughed with her but, Samantha noted, the seriousness never disappeared from her eyes. "There you are, Samantha," she said, resuming their conversation. "You've been warned about him. Do you want the job?"

Sam wasn't concerned. Her specialty was handling ornery patients. "I'll take it."

* * *

Sam had planned to meet Max Montgomery before his discharge date, but the two times she'd stopped by his room, he'd been off somewhere for tests.

So their first meeting came on the day he was to go home. While the doctor checked him out one last time, Sam waited at the nurses' station with a wheelchair. When the doctor left the room, she wheeled the chair into it.

It was one thing to see Max Montgomery from a distance—in the bank, he'd looked formidable in his gray banker's suit—but up close, he tongue-tied her. Six-feet-plus, lean and muscular, he was drop-dead gorgeous with an aristocratic nose and high cheekbones. Quite simply, he had movie star good looks.

Rachel was standing in front of a portable table near the bed, packing personal items into a bag. "Father should be here," she said.

Sitting on the bed, Max stared blankly out the window, toward the statue of Lewis and Clark outside the hospital entrance. A second passed before he rounded a look at his sister. "I might have lost my memory, but it doesn't take much to get the picture. You're about to make excuses for him, aren't you? Did you always do that?"

Sam thought she noted a flicker of hope enter Rachel's eyes as she looked at her brother. As if she recognized his abrupt, no-nonsense attitude as a familiar one for Max, making him seem like the man she knew.

"No, we never tried to fool each other about him."

"Then don't start now."

Rachel visibly relaxed. "Okay."

Standing at the doorway, Sam cleared her throat to be noticed.

"Hi." Rachel smiled a greeting. "I'm glad you got here."

Sam pushed the wheelchair farther into the room. "I thought I'd come and take over."

"That would be great. I left Alyssa—"

"Hold it." A masculine voice demanded their attention. "Who are you?" His eyes snapped with annoyance at Sam. "And what did you mean by 'take over'?"

Sam geared up for his resistance and planted her feet. "I'm Samantha Carter. Rachel—"

"What's that for?" He jabbed a hand at the air in the direction of the wheelchair. "I don't need it."

"Then we'll be staying here," Sam replied. "Because they're not letting you escape until you climb into this."

He eyed her with a look meant to back her out the door. "What's with the 'we'?"

Sam had hoped for a better beginning. "I'm your private nurse," she said, negotiating the wheelchair closer to the bed.

He shot a glance in Rachel's direction. "Is that true?"

"Max, you need someone to stay with you. And you don't have the cook anymore or the housekeeper."

"Why don't I?"

Though Sam empathized with his confusion, she guessed any softness with him at this moment would be her downfall. "I've been told you annoyed the cook for the last time. And no one knows why the housekeeper left."

Rachel held her lips in a tight line, looking as if she was having trouble holding back a smile. "I'll leave, and have the car brought around."

"I have mine here," Sam told her. "It would be best if we take it."

"Okay. I'll go to the desk and make sure he's discharged." She breezed out the door before anyone could respond.

Though he glared, Max swung his legs over the side of the bed. Sam braked the chair and reached for his arm. "Let me help."

"I can do this myself."

She found herself pinned by steel-blue eyes. Unfriendly eyes.

"I don't need a nursemaid."

Patience had always been one of Sam's best traits. "You're not getting one."

"Good," he snapped, and grasped the arm of the wheelchair.

Sam admired his independence. He'd be a difficult patient, not because he didn't have the courage required in therapy, but because he would battle her all the way.

He slouched back in the chair, tiredness etching deeper lines in his face.

Sam stared at the cast that ran across the top of his hand to his bicep. Usually, little notes of encouragement were scribbled on a cast, but not a pen had touched his.

It was as immaculately white as when it was first applied.

Giving him time to recover, she busied herself with the bag Rachel had packed. He'd proven what he wanted. Hopefully he would now accept her help.

A strained quiet stretched between them on the ride in the elevator. When they reached the sidewalk in front of the hospital, Rachel left them, promising to call after dinner. Max remained silent, and Sam wondered how long it would continue.

She opened the passenger door of her car. Recalling the BMW he'd tooled around town in, she guessed her five-year-old, four-wheel drive wouldn't receive a passing grade with any Montgomery.

Once he was settled on the passenger's seat, she grabbed the seat belt clip and leaned across him to snap the buckle. She'd done the same action dozens of times with other patients, but somehow this was different. Max was…disturbing. With his face mere inches from hers, with the heat of his breath caressing her face, sensation sprinted through her.

Do the job. Get done. Move away, her brain ordered even as her pulse scrambled. Her heart pounding harder, Sam fumbled with the belt buckle. It took two tries, and all the while his breath caressed her cheek.

Daring a look at him, she watched his gaze idly roam over her face. Lined up, their lips were a mere hairbreadth apart. There was danger here, she recognized. Far more for her than him.

"Are you done?" he asked.

Too long. Too long she'd leaned across him, stayed close. Unwavering, his stare challenged every feminine instinct within her. But it was his mouth, the firm, sensual line of his lips, that played havoc with her woman's sensibility. "Yes." Backing out of the car, she shut his door and, moving quickly, rounded the front. She definitely needed to keep her mind on business.

"Don't I have a car?" he asked the moment she slid behind the steering wheel.

Sam gave a grateful sigh that he was willing to treat those previous seconds as if they'd never happened. "You were in better shape than it was after the accident." She switched on the ignition. The engine cranked and died. "You don't remember the accident?" She knew differently. According to his hospital chart which she'd read earlier, the doctor had noted that the patient recalled the accident. He could also identify the composers of certain music, authors of books, sports teams, the names of planets. But not the names of family and friends. Sam turned the key again. This time the engine purred. With partial amnesia, patients often remembered some things and not others.

"I remember the accident," he finally answered.

"What exactly do you remember?"

Silence answered her. Obviously he'd exhausted his willingness to converse with her. Head turned away, he stared out the window. Sam left him alone and negotiated the Jeep onto the street. She had a tendency to talk too much sometimes, a habit she was aware some people might view as a fault.

With the plopping of raindrops against the window, she started the windshield wipers. She'd have liked to turn on a CD, something bluesy, maybe the wailing sounds of "Smoke Gets in Your Eyes," but not knowing if Max hated blues, she mentally hummed the song.

Before this job ended, she would learn his likes and dislikes. Being a private nurse meant getting as close to a patient as a family member or a spouse. "Let's see. Your sister said to turn here." She knew who owned the mansion on the hill. Everyone did. But to get to the private drive that led to his home, she'd needed directions from Rachel.

As the rain slowed, Sam rolled down her window. She liked the smell of rain, the cool dampness that lingered in the air after it stopped. She wasn't alone, it seemed.

As they traveled the road to his private drive, they passed a neighbor's property. Despite the drizzle, a couple had walked to their mailbox. For a while his neighbors would be her neighbors. Sam waved, planning to meet them later.

No one waved back. Rather than unfriendly, Sam viewed their response as puzzled and wondered just how many of his neighbors Max Montgomery had offended.

Perhaps plenty of them, she reasoned, based on the Keep Out and No Trespassing signs posted on the security gate at the entrance to his property. He was definitely big on privacy. "Is there a security code?"

Slowly he angled a look at her. "Wasn't that your business to find out?"

With some effort, Sam delivered her sweetest smile. "Yes, it was." This wasn't pleasant or easy for him, she reminded herself. She'd been a nurse long enough to know that a patient's crankiness directed at her was rarely personal. After braking, she shifted to park, then retrieved her cell phone from her shoulder bag. To her relief, Rachel answered immediately. "We're at a loss," Sam told her. "Neither of us knows the security code." Still talking to Rachel, Sam left the car to punch in the code.

A born optimist, she delivered a pep talk to herself before returning to the car. Once she and Max were settled in, everything would go more smoothly.

That might not be true, she immediately realized when she returned to the car and her passenger finally spoke. "When we get to the house, take my bag in. Then leave."

Because he sounded as if he believed she'd do what he'd said, Sam insisted, "I'll be staying."

His gaze sliced to her. He had devastating eyes—eyes that would cut people down with one look. "I don't care that my—that Rachel hired you," he said, seeming to have a problem calling her his sister. "I don't want you." He gave her that superior look she imagined he'd learned at an early age. "I'm firing you, Ms...."

"Samantha—Sam Carter." Sam pushed strands of damp hair out of her eyes. "Mr. Montgomery, let's get something straight. I'm not your maid, I'm not your housekeeper and I am not your servant. I am your nurse."

"What if I don't want you?"

"That's not an option." Sam shrugged indifferently. "For a while you're stuck with a nurse. For tonight, it's me. If you want someone else, you'll have to talk to your sister. But I don't think that will do any good. Whether you like it or not, I can't leave."

She also couldn't take her eyes off the house. Nothing had prepared her for his home. She caught herself gaping as she stared at the view between the slow-swishing windshield wipers. He lived in a brick-and-terra-cotta Tudor-style mansion, grand and impressive, especially with the darkening sky above it and the lightning casting the outside in bizarre illumination.

"Why won't it do any good to talk to my sister?"

It took a moment before Sam realized he'd returned to their previous conversation. "Because your reputation is well known," she answered honestly. She'd gone into nursing because of a need to help others, because of a desire to comfort, but that didn't mean she couldn't be tough if it was in her patient's best interest. "It means no one else will work for you. I was Rachel's last hope."

"Why you?"

"That's easy to answer." Sam took a leveling breath. "I make it a point to take care of one grump a year. You're it." She cast a sidelong glance at Mr. Bank President to see how he handled that remark. There was the slightest curve at the edges of his lips, as if he might smile. Couldn't be, she mused. Everyone knew Max Montgomery never smiled.

Two

She'd made him smile. That was something Max hadn't felt like doing since he'd awakened at the hospital. She also irritated the hell out of him. And she was getting under his skin in another way.

With her closeness during her efforts with the seat belt, a flowery fragrance had curled around him. He'd noticed the pulse at her throat quickening. Then the side of her breast had brushed his chest when she'd stretched across him.

He'd been aware of her. Say it like it was, he told himself. His mind might be running on fewer cylinders, but his body had heated up just fine.

Bringing himself back to his surroundings, he stared in disbelief at the house. *His* house. The rain stopped, giving him a clear view. "This is it?" It confirmed what he'd gathered during conversations with his family and from comments made by the hospital staff. He was rich.

"Yes, this is your house." Sam removed the ignition key, then opened her door and reached for his bag from the back seat. "Does it seem familiar?"

Max shook his head.

Nothing did. The bag contained his razor and shaving cream and toothbrush, and several magazines. Everything Rachel had brought him could have belonged to someone else. Nothing had triggered any memory. Not this house, either. His stomach clenched. What if everything inside looked strange and unfamiliar?

He'd like to stay in the car, tell the cheerful redhead who now stood beside his door to drive him anywhere, to just get him away from the house. Instead, she opened the door for him and held out a hand. "I've been in museums that were smaller," he said. He brushed away her hand, not wanting her help. But ignoring her was impossible.

Trim, tall, probably nearing thirty, she possessed a knock-out figure, well-toned, with long legs. The whole package dazzled him, from the generous mouth to the laughing green eyes and the riot of red hair with its abundance of curls to her shoulders.

Her face was the delicate, fine-boned one of a Celtic beauty, with a pert nose and a flawless, pale complexion. He couldn't say he wouldn't enjoy staring at that face or that body under different circumstances. But no matter what she looked like or how well she was put together, or how much she fired up the ache in his gut, he didn't want her here, didn't like what that bright smile of hers made him feel.

"Do you remember going to a museum?" she asked.

He considered not answering her. He supposed her job included daily reports on his memory to the doctor or to Ellis or to some shrink. But he nodded in response. "Yes. And a planetarium." How old had he been when he was there? In the museum, had he been looking at the model train station with a child's eyes or a man's? Damn. Why were memories so elusive? He felt as if he was in limbo, not connected to anything, even himself.

"Are you remembering something else?"

Enough questions. He maneuvered himself out of the car. She stood only inches from him now, and he saw the sprinkling of freckles on the bridge of her nose, neatly camouflaged by makeup. It would make more sense if he didn't notice anything about her. "Who's going to clean this?" he asked with a nod in the direction of the house.

Briefly she made eye contact with him. Don't suggest that I do it, her look silently conveyed. "Not me." The house keys dangling from her fingers, she pivoted away and glided toward the front door.

Max didn't miss her smile. Not for the first time, he thought that smile might buckle a man's knees. Trailing her to the door, he swept a slow, appraising look at the grounds. Well-kept, manicured. Obviously the handiwork of a diligent gardener. A flower garden of pink and white flowers lined the walkway. He counted eight huge trees in the front of the property, eyed the woods that backed the house.

The house pleased him, he realized, though he thought the brass lion's head door knocker was ostentatious. He assumed it was part of the package when he'd bought the house.

Moving closer, he noticed that she'd frozen in the opened doorway. "What's the problem?"

"No problem. Look." With a sweep of her arm, she directed his gaze to the wall of paintings that adorned the stairway wall. "Monet, Cezanne. Do you know if those are real?"

Max remained behind her. More than the paintings grabbed his attention. Her knowledge surprised him. "I have no idea," he said, wondering just how educated she was. The allure of her perfume enticing him again, he dodged contact and quickly brushed past her.

With a lengthy look, he scanned his surroundings, assessed the grandfather clock, an antique-looking table. What was a genuine antique and what wasn't? This was his home, he reminded himself, yet he felt no familiarity with it. Where was his room, his things? Panic threaded through him again. Instead of answers, questions flooded his mind. "Why exactly don't I have a housekeeper?"

Her back to him, his Florence Nightingale stroked a crystal vase that was on the foyer table. "According to your sister—Rachel, you sent the housekeeper off in tears."

"Why?"

"I told you. I don't know."

It was probably best to not know, Max decided. He might not like the answer. He crossed the gleaming dark-stained floor and halted at the staircase. To his left was a paneled library. To his right was a living room, complete with a deep blue sofa and a floor-to-ceiling bay window. A mahogany piano occupied one corner. He wondered if he played. "Let's go," he said, aware she hadn't yet moved. "You had directions how to get here. Did you also learn which room is mine?"

She smirked at him with a look, one he could only interpret as "Gotcha." "Well, Watson, logic would tell us it's the biggest."

The amusement in her voice irked him. Max leveled a glare at her, not caring to admit he deserved that. "Are you always so cheerful, or is this an act for my benefit?"

Sliding the straps of his bag over her shoulder, Sam whisked past him and started up the stairs. "*I* try to be pleasant."

What was left unsaid came through clearly. What's your excuse for being so disagreeable? He could have told her. *You.*

Max watched her hips sway as she climbed the stairs ahead of him. He may not know squat about himself but he knew a certain edginess whenever she stood too near. What will it take to make her leave? he wondered. At the second-floor landing, he trailed her to the end of the hallway.

Huge was his first thought when he entered the room. A masculine room of dark wood, it was decorated in navy and deep burgundy colors. Staring at the brass deer that stood beside a mahogany writing desk, Max assumed Rachel or an interior designer had used a free hand in decorating the house. He didn't think he would have a knack for it.

But then what the hell did he know? This was his room and nothing looked familiar. Nothing clicked a switch in his mind. Eyes squeezed shut, he stood in the middle of the room. *Think, damn it. Think. Open your eyes. Remember something. Anything.*

At the thump behind him, he snapped open his eyes and looked back to see Samantha standing in the doorway where she'd dropped his bag.

"I'll unpack that for you in a little while."

He wanted to be alone. He wanted time to think, to explore, to touch. Something in the house had to bring back his past.

"Be back in a moment." She gave him that quick smile of hers.

It annoyed him. *She* annoyed him. She was too helpful. "Where are you going?"

"To find my space."

Another person would have said room, Max thought. He'd have guessed she was a free spirit. Someone with all that untamed red hair couldn't be the type easily contained. And him—what had he been like? A bank president. Sounded stuffy. Was he a boring man, one of those pencil pushers who lived for his work? What did he like to do when he wasn't at work?

With a turn, he saw his reflection in the mirror. A stranger stared back at him. He noted that he was muscled. From lifting weights or from some other physical activity? He stared into the steel-blue eyes and saw nothing. Just like what was in his head: nothing. Scowling, he turned away from the image.

From another room, he heard whistling. She didn't annoy him. She aggravated him. He dropped to the edge of the mattress and listened, trying to name the melody. Offhand, he couldn't.

The sound of sneakered feet, hurrying along the hallway, then down the stairs, preceded the slam of the door. She was *not* quiet.

Max wanted to go to sleep, to sleep until he was normal again. He flopped back onto the bed and stared at the ceiling. So he was home. Now what? He couldn't carry on as if nothing was wrong and act normal. He didn't know what normal was.

Samantha left him alone. They'd have to work their way through this initial awkward period. Eventually Max would realize he did need her. In the meantime, they were living together. She wasn't the least bit worried about handling him. She'd developed resilience and optimism to combat any adversary, even one who was a tall, dark, handsome grump.

From the eight guest bedrooms, she chose a cream-colored room with a similar-colored bedspread and area rug. Tiny pink roses bordered the edges of the eyelet throw pillows. Though the room was smaller than the others, it was closest to his. The room was airy and had an upholstered chair to relax in and a writing desk.

As she'd lugged her suitcases up the stairs, she'd noticed the abundance of chandeliers, the stained- and leaded-glass windows, the stone fireplaces. Planning to unpack later, she left her bags in her room and wandered back down the stairs. She ambled through a library and a sunroom with a fountain.

She loved the honey-colored oak floors in the bedrooms, and here in the living room with its vaulted ceiling, exposed beams and stone fireplace.

She thought she'd died and gone to heaven when she came across the kitchen with its teak cabinetry, brick floor and butler's pantry. Even before she'd brought in her bags, she'd been itching to get into the kitchen, eager to cook something.

Because Rachel had promised to hire someone by the end of the week to do the cleaning and laundry, Samantha had agreed to do the cooking until a cook could be hired. Sam had known she'd have the time, since her patient would require minimal care. Chock-full of nervous energy, she'd never been a couch potato or television addict, the thought of preparing meals was a welcome one.

In passing through the huge dining room, she'd rescued several wilting plants and carried them with her into the kitchen. Setting them in the sink, she fingered the drooping leaf of a philodendron on the kitchen windowsill. Because she was away from home so much, she had no pet or plants. It would be fun to nurture this one and the others.

Spotting a radio in a corner, she flicked on a favorite station. To the sultry sound of "Mood Indigo," Sam made coffee, then inventoried the contents of the refrigerator, freezer and the pantry. As promised during a phone conversation, Rachel had done some grocery shopping. Spotting thawed ground beef, Sam came up with a quick dinner idea for their first meal. After she slid the meat loaf into the oven, she peeled potatoes for pan roasting, then climbed the steps to Max's room.

It was empty.

She searched through the bedrooms on the second floor. Steps from a closed bathroom door, she heard his curse. One word. Loud. A person of lesser courage would take the expletive as a warning to stay clear. Sam marched forward and knocked on the door, ready to deal with his crisis. "Need help?"

The bathroom door flung open. Happy, he wasn't. "You keep saying that to annoy me, don't you?"

Sam managed a smile. "I say it because that's what I'm being paid to do. Help you. What's the problem?"

He held up the arm in the cast. "I give." He turned the scowl that had been directed on her to the stuck zipper of his jeans.

Challenge number one, Sam decided. "Material is stuck."

"No kidding."

Sam narrowed her eyes at him. She could leave him like this. No, she couldn't. This had to be embarrassing for him. Stepping near, she reached down and tugged at the denim stuck in the teeth of the zipper. She felt the bulge against her knuckles. The heat. The hardening. And she heard him suck in a breath. "I think I've got it." She gritted her teeth and tugged at the denim. She'd kill herself if she blushed like some adolescent. "There. Your—" Her voice died.

Though not a hand touched her, she looked up and was trapped by that steely gaze. Something fluttered within her. "Your sister left a list of what you like to eat." She wished her legs felt as firm as her voice sounded.

"Like what?"

"Like—" She was certain he stood closer. A lot closer. "I need to go. Check on it."

What she needed was a moment alone, time to think clearly. He didn't cooperate. She heard his footsteps behind her on the stairs.

"You didn't tell me what you're cooking."

A trace of amusement in his voice caused her to falter in mid-stride as she entered the kitchen. Was he having a laugh at her expense? Sam turned a speculative look on him. He looked deadly serious. There wasn't even an inkling of a smile. She must have been wrong, she decided. "Meat loaf."

He grimaced. "Save me." He flicked off the radio, abruptly ending a jazzy piano version of "Blue Moon."

Sam sighed with exasperation. Poison might work.

She laughed at her own thought and flung open the freezer door to remove a package of frozen strawberries.

"Is that your best offer?"

She disregarded what sounded like a deliberate sarcastic goad. "Actually it isn't. I could whip up great tamales, spinach enchiladas, beef and broccoli stir fry, fettuccine alfredo. I worked for a lady who loved to cruise and took me with her when she traveled. While with her, I lived in a home in Acapulco. I studied how to make the Mexican cook's fabulous dishes." Her smile firmly in place, Sam pivoted toward him. "Do you like Mexican food? Because if you do, I'll make something like that one night."

"You talk a lot."

Leaning his shoulder against the doorjamb, he studied her with that narrowed, deciphering look.

"I've been told that before." Distance from him had helped. Feeling less unsettled, she turned on the sink spigot and let water rush over the frozen package of fruit. Never before had she intimidated easily. She smiled with a fond memory of a Fortune 500 CEO. Stuck in traction, he'd barked orders constantly and had never fazed her. "Did you rest at all?"

"Too much in the hospital." He circled the kitchen, opening and closing cupboards.

"I doubt if you're familiar with this room."

"Why not?"

"You're a wealthy man, Mr. Montgomery." She opened the package of strawberries and dumped the fruit in a bowl. "Wealthy people don't usually hang out in the kitchen."

"What do wealthy people do?"

Again she thought she heard humor in his voice. It didn't matter if he was having fun at her expense. In fact, she hoped he was. He needed to let loose a little. "They play tennis. They go swimming." She thought the answer to his question was obvious since there was a kidney-shaped pool at the back of the house.

"Hardly." He held up the arm in the cast. "Busted wing."

"I didn't mean at this moment. It's raining." Sam sent him an easy smile. "Do you like to walk in it? I do."

He shrugged and ambled to the window. "Who knows?" He motioned toward the table in front of the bay window that was set for one. On top of a hunter-green-and-burgundy-patterned place mat, she'd placed a matching napkin, a hunter-green dinner plate and a water goblet. "Aren't you eating?"

"That is for me," Sam said.

"And me?" An obstinate tone entered his voice. "I'm not eating in bed."

She'd never considered the idea, but felt a tease rise within her. "People of leisure often eat in bed."

"Are you enjoying yourself?"

She actually thought she saw him grin. "Pardon?"

"Carter, is aggravating me part of the therapy?"

She couldn't hold back a laugh. "Of course not."

"Then quit the mumbo jumbo and answer my question."

"Actually, you never asked one. You told me you weren't eating in bed. I never thought you would. I set the dining room table for you."

"Alone?"

Sam would have preferred company. During other jobs, she'd usually eaten with the person in her care, had been treated not as a servant or an employee but as a companion. But she wasn't quite sure of her position with Max Montgomery.

"Forget that idea. We'll eat together. Here or there."

"I'd like that." She said the words to his back. "I'd prefer here. It's less formal."

Idly he scanned the room. "Suits me. When will dinner be ready?"

"In a few minutes. But if you want to rest—"

"I don't."

Feeling as if they'd made headway, Sam ignored the curtness in his voice. "Your sister said you lost weight while in the hospital. Everyone does."

She looked up from the bowl of strawberries and saw him wandering toward the French door. As he opened it and stepped outside onto the patio, she concentrated on finishing the meal preparation. What hurt does he harbor? she wondered. From what she'd heard about him, he'd been a distant man. He'd also suffered a recent tragedy, the death of his younger sister. Sam wondered if anyone had told him about that since he'd regained consciousness. She needed to find out. She certainly didn't want to say something about Christina Montgomery if he had no idea who she was and what had happened to her.

Sam clicked on the radio again, feeling more at ease with music around her. In between steaming string beans and unrolling a package of crescent biscuits, she danced around the kitchen. Singing "Fever" along with Peggy Lee, she gave a final bump and grind and whirled around.

And saw him standing in the doorway. Rain glistened on his hair, a soft misty sheen clung to his skin.

Inwardly she tensed. Deep-set eyes were locked on her. Without doing anything but looking at her, he unsettled her. He skittered sensation through her. She took in a deep breath and tried to ignore the pressure in her chest, the quickened beat of her heart. "You're wet." Brilliant comment, she berated herself.

Her pulse still beating fast, she watched him run his hand over his damp face, then turn away. Alone, she leaned against the counter. It didn't matter that she was attracted to him, that he sparked desire. Max Montgomery had to be off limits.

Dinner was a silent affair. Sam waited for him to take as much as he wanted from the serving platters and bowls, then she cut the food into bite-size portions for him. He looked pained by his limitations. While he could feed himself and she imagined he'd have no problem with bathing except for out-of-reach places such as his back, he needed her help somewhat. From their initial encounter, she'd gathered that he hated depending on anyone for anything.

She'd tried—she'd honestly tried—to engage him in conversation when they'd first sat down. But after receiving a dozen monosyllabic answers from him, she'd given up. She'd resigned herself to silent meals when midway through the dinner, he broke the silence.

"Meat loaf is hamburger," he said suddenly.

What was his point? she wondered. "Don't Montgomerys eat hamburger?"

"You tell me."

"I assure you that Mayor Ellis Montgomery will devour his share of hot dogs and hamburgers while on the campaign trail." Noticing his empty cup, Sam nudged back her chair to get the coffeepot. "You do know about his political plans?"

He only nodded. Sam resolved to have some kind of conversation with him, even if it was mostly one-sided. "Do you remember your mother?" she went on while she filled their coffee cups. To her pleasure, he took another slice of meat loaf from the serving plate.

"No, I don't." He poked his fork into a potato chunk. "Who knows why?"

Sam didn't buy his cavalier attitude. What he was going through was frightening. His past had been erased. He had no emotional ties because he couldn't remember them. To another patient, she might have tried to talk about the amnesia and bring out feelings. But sensing how private he was, she thought he would need time to be ready for that.

Despite his claim not to like her meat loaf or the pan-roasted potatoes, he devoured two helpings. While he ate a huge serving of the strawberry shortcake, Sam cleared away their dinner plates.

"Why don't you work at a hospital?" he asked out of the blue.

Pleased he'd initiated conversation this time, Sam took a seat across the table from him again. She noticed that he looked tired. The first day home often was the hardest. "I like working one-on-one with a patient," she explained. "And I have more freedom this way."

"I'd think you'd have less. You're stuck here. At a hospital, you'd leave when your shift is over and go home."

"But the shift would be the same hours every day. One lady I worked for liked to get up at five in the morning, take a four-hour nap in the afternoon, and stay up until two."

A frown creased a line between his brows. "You liked that?"

"It was fun for a while. And then there was an elderly man recovering from a hip replacement who lived five days a week in Phoenix and two at a cabin in the woods. He always was on the go."

Max didn't want to be interested, but she doled out just enough information to make him curious. "You lived in Arizona?"

"And California and Colorado." She paused to sip the hot brew. "I came here five years ago."

"From where originally?"

"Oklahoma. Well, not exactly. My mama fell for a cowboy with an Oklahoma twang when I was three and we moved there from Kansas. Then she met a fellow who thought he was the next Waylon Jennings, and we moved to Nashville."

What looked like curiosity sprang into his eyes. "With him?"

"Yes." Sam usually didn't tell so much about her personal life to a patient. Well, that wasn't really true. Usually she waited until she'd been working for the person at least a week; by then, she was good friends with them. Over the rim of her coffee cup, she found herself the recipient of another frown. It might take longer than a week with Max, but she'd turn him around.

"Why did you stay in Whitehorn if you have no family here?"

Sam went to the sink. "I loved the country," she said over the rush of water as she rinsed a plate. "Like you."

"Like me?"

Over her shoulder, she saw his frown deepen to a scowl. "I heard you've lived in a lot of places, but you settled here," she said.

"Because of work, I moved around." Max had gotten that information from Ellis—his father. He felt no strong affection for the man and wondered if he ever had. He'd felt different when Rachel had visited him in the hospital, had been glad to see her.

"Are you remembering something?"

A moment passed before he snapped himself back. "I came here because of my work."

"Yes, but—" She paused, took in the view beyond the bay window. "Look at this scenery. You could have lived anywhere, but you chose to live on a hill that gave an eagle's view of the country." She stalled until he shifted toward the window, then persisted to keep the conversation going. "This is so beautiful," she said. "I think this is why you're really here. Who wouldn't love this." Sam waited only a second. It didn't matter to her that he hadn't responded. She wasn't giving up. "I noticed a piano in the other room."

"If you can play, go ahead." Cautiously he drank his coffee. "And before you ask, I'll tell you that I don't know if I play."

"I can't, though I always wanted to play a musical instrument. But as a child, my mother never had the money, and as an adult, I never seemed to have the time. I bet you play."

He finished off the last of the food on the plate in front of him. "Why?"

"Because you're not the type of man to have something just for the sake of appearance. You're too practical." With a look she interpreted as deciphering, he leaned back in his chair. "What?" she asked, feeling as if she were under a microscope.

"Nothing." Amazing, Max mused. He didn't know a thing about himself, and she'd come up with that. Was her analysis of him accurate? Damn, why was he believing what some stranger said to him?

"This was really rather pleasant, wasn't it?"

He saw such delight in her expression. Staring into eyes that were sparkling with a smile, he felt something slow and warming travel through him. "Don't let it go to your head," he quipped.

She laughed. "I'm sure you won't let me."

* * *

Alone, later, Max climbed the steps and went into the bathroom adjacent to the master suite. Having shed his shirt and pants, he eyed the tub in the corner. It was big enough for four, as was the walk-in shower.

During dinner, she'd mentioned his taking a shower and said something about a plastic covering for the heavy cast on his arm. In the hospital, he'd put up with sponge baths by women old enough to be his grandmother.

He'd realized then, when he'd felt no self-consciousness, that he was comfortable being naked in front of a woman. But he couldn't recollect past love interests. It seemed a shame to have no memory of them.

Not that he'd felt even a twinge of desire around the sourpuss named Nurse Schmidt who had wheeled him to the hospital shower. In fact, she or someone else wheeled him everywhere even though nothing had been wrong with his legs.

He'd admit that bathing wasn't easy with only one arm, but he'd mastered a workable technique—except for his back. The chirpy Ms. Carter would get that job.

For his own peace of mind, he decided to limit how much she helped him. That was best since he thought too much about her as it was. More than once, hadn't he noticed how well she moved? All through dinner he'd been unable to get the image of her dancing out of his head, the sway of her hips, the subtle bounce of her breasts.

At the knock on the door, he turned on the taps to

adjust the water. If he kept thinking the same way, he would need a cold shower. "Come in."

"Do you want to shower tonight or…?"

He heard her steps slow on the tiled floor. He didn't need to answer her. He dropped his briefs and stood with his bare back to her.

"You need a plastic wrap on your cast."

Max pivoted back at the same moment that she crossed to him. Briefly her eyes strayed to his bare chest, then swept up to squarely meet his stare. He figured she noticed plenty. So had he. With her close now, he couldn't ignore her scent. A fantasy danced in his head of her naked, wet, in the shower with him, all that red hair curling even more in the dampness.

As she stretched around him to turn off the water and connect a hoselike spray attachment to the shower head, he held still. He was far from calm and cool. It occurred to him that if he leaned an inch or two closer to her she wouldn't need to guess what he was thinking; his body would give away his thoughts.

With a step back, Sam held out the plastic covering she'd brought in with her. Seconds later, she'd wrapped the plastic around the cast. "Spray first."

Cursing, Max moved around her and into the shower stall. She was killing his ego, he decided. He wasn't certain what he was looking for. Anything except what he viewed as her blasé attitude.

He'd learned something else about himself. When naked with a woman, he preferred to be the one in control. He sat on the stool she'd positioned in the shower and sprayed water over his body and down his back.

Tension lasted only another second. Inch by inch, his body began to relax as she rubbed a soft, sudsy cloth in slow circles along his wet shoulders. She had great hands. Soft but strong. And gentle fingers. They kneaded his shoulders through the soapy washcloth. One by one, the muscles in his back loosened beneath her gentle manipulations.

Relaxed, he closed his eyes, and his head fell back. Water dripped from it. He felt her hands in his hair, massaging.

"Mr. Montgomery?"

He could barely think, much less talk. Mentally he laughed as his mind registered what she'd said. He was naked, and she was calling him "mister."

"Do you want me to wash your legs and feet?"

To have her hands on him any longer might be disastrous. "No." He shook his head for good measure. "Go."

"I'll be in the other room if you need me."

Max didn't respond, couldn't. The moment she stepped away, he pushed to a stand. She'd left the shower door open and he looked out, saw her drape an oversize towel on top of the nearby black wicker hamper.

As the bathroom door closed behind her, he collapsed against the cool tile. Damn. She definitely wasn't on the same plane as the granite-faced, old biddy Nurse Schmidt.

Three

A good night's sleep helped. Max felt better than he had in a week though the cast on his arm meant no on-the-belly sleeping. And despite what he might not remember, he sensed he would feel most comfortable that way.

Yawning, he inched his way out of bed, then walked to the double closet. When he heard the knock on the bedroom door, he considered not answering, but he figured Samantha would just walk right in. "Come in."

Ms. Sunshine breezed in wearing a bright yellow Henley shirt that hung to the edge of her hips. On the right side of the three-button neckline was finger-size stitching of Sylvester the Cat. Snug jeans and snow-white sneakers completed the less than nurselike ensemble. "I brought you a glass of O.J. and coffee as long as I was coming up."

Even more than before, he'd prefer that she'd leave. She'd been on his mind before he'd fallen asleep. She'd been on his mind first thing this morning. He didn't care for the feelings she'd stirred within him yesterday when the zipper had stuck, and then during the shower. And he didn't need a nurse, especially her, hovering around him. "When are you going?"

She set down the tray, then over her shoulder, she flashed him one of her hundred-watt smiles. "I'm wearing my garlic necklace today to ward off evil spirits, so nothing you do will frighten me off."

"You're a real kick, Carter."

"I'll take that as a compliment." Again the big smile. "Thank you. Have you decided on clothes for today?"

He pegged her as stubborn not dense. "Just got here."

She came up behind him at the closet. "Expensive threads. As a banker, it makes sense you'd have so many suits," she said as she pushed at hangers and scrutinized each suit.

Max was still taking all of them in. There was a closetful of sedate gray and dark-colored suits, starched dress shirts, an abundance of ties. All of them were conservative in color, too. More than half a dozen dress shoes were lined up in a row. Someone had polished them to a gleaming shine.

"We know one thing. You're a clotheshorse. You've got enough suits to outfit an army. Black, gray, pin-stripes. Ah, what color is this? Olive, maybe," she said, examining the sleeve of the jacket.

He had to admit there was more than he'd expected.

"But what about casual knock-around-and-watch-television type clothes?" She came around him to his left. "There we are," she said with satisfaction. "More jeans. Worn-looking ones. And hiking boots. You like to hike."

Did he?

"I found a man's rain slicker in a downstairs closet off the kitchen. Bet you like to fish in the rain. So what looks comfortable to you, or do you want to stay in those?" she said with a gesture toward the gray sweatpants he'd worn to bed.

"I'll get dressed." He scanned the clothes, touched the collar of a shirt.

"What are you doing?"

He answered because he sensed she'd keep at him until he did. "Checking the label to learn my size."

A look flashed into her eyes, one of sympathy. He didn't want it or anything else from her. Looking away, he fingered the sleeve of a faded blue plaid shirt.

"I'd say that's a good shirt. Pick your most unfavorite shirt. I might have to open up the seam just above the cuff to get it over the cast."

Max kept his fingers on the blue one.

He decided she was a touch loony. The shirt looked faded and old to him.

"If I were you, I'd choose a different one," she said.

Max considered arguing, but decided it took too much effort and snagged a newer-looking shirt from a hanger. "Does this one get your approval?" Now that she'd backed away, he no longer pulled in her scent with each breath he took and could think more clearly.

Giving the shirt a long, steady look, she shrugged. "Who knows for sure?"

"Then why not the blue one?"

"It's old looking."

"Ready to be thrown out," Max said.

"More likely it's your favorite, one you kept around long past its time. Wouldn't you hate to get your memory back and learn you ruined your favorite shirt?"

As she took off, Max stared after her. He might be losing it. She was actually beginning to make sense to him.

Alone, he tugged down first one side of his sweatpants, then the other. Determined, he contorted to get briefs on. Every act required an enormous amount of energy.

Sitting on the edge of the mattress, the jeans pooled on the floor by his bare feet, he took a breather. He remembered how eager he'd been to get out of the hospital, so sure he would need no one hanging around. Standing, he worked the denim up, and with disgust, he stared down at the metal buttons on the fly. He'd been wrong. He needed someone.

In response to the sound of footsteps, he looked up. With her return, a nervous edge rippled through him again. As he sat, she dropped to her knees in front of him to slip on first one sock and then the other. He hated this, hated the idea of leaning on anyone for anything, being needy.

And he wasn't fond of the feelings she sparked

within him. While she tied his sneakers, sunlight danced across the top of her hair. Golden strands mingled with the red. He wanted to reach out, touch her hair, feel the silkiness between his fingers.

"Okay. If you stand, I'll button your jeans."

How nonchalant she sounded. Damn it, it wasn't fair. He was dying inside, heat humming through him, and there she was, looking cool and unaffected.

With each button she touched, with each brush of her fingers, his body tensed. A second, then two passed of too much sensation swamping him. Feeling as if he were being punched hard in the midsection, he kept a firm control on himself. But what about tomorrow morning? Or the next? This wasn't going to work. He needed Nurse Schmidt, the crab of Whitehorn Memorial's Medical/Surgical Unit.

"I'll make breakfast now." She stepped back, never looking at him. "Would you like to have it on the patio?"

He recalled that beyond the patio was a well-mani-cured lawn and a flower garden bright with color, mostly pinks and white and yellow. "What's for break-fast?"

"I make a mean omelet." Sam waited for a response. Instead he offered his back to her. Maybe that was best.

She left and hurried toward the kitchen. Like last night, this morning with him had tested her. Try as she might to remain unaffected by closeness with him, she was not made of stone.

An underlying current, that intangible thing—chemistry or whatever—existed between them. Seeing him half naked again reminded her of those moments before his shower when he'd bared all. She'd admired the play of muscles in his broad back, and the taut backside. In fact, it was the best-looking tush she'd ever seen. It surprised her that he was a physically tough-looking man with broad shoulders and strong arms. He should have been soft, sitting behind a desk all the time, but he had a hard, muscled body.

Before she'd slipped the plastic protection over his cast, she'd noticed—how could she not?—the well-formed muscles in his arms and chest, the flat rippled midsection, and more.

As a professional, she never forgot the advice an older nurse had given her—to not become emotionally involved with a patient. Sometimes Sam didn't follow the advice, but she'd never had this particular problem before. Caring for her patients was one thing. Lusting for one of them was quite another.

Perhaps this was her own fault. She'd been without a man in her life for so long, naturally he'd tempt her. After all, hadn't he been unofficially declared Whitehorn's best-looking male by a majority of the town's females? So of course, he tripped her heart a little. But what she needed was a vacation, not him in her life. Maybe a summer fling somewhere exotic like Cancun, anywhere but Whitehorn.

Determined to think about anything else, she puttered around the kitchen, first setting the table on the patio, then gathering everything for an omelet. With the bread in the toaster slots, the eggs whisked and ready to slide into the pan, she poured herself a cup of coffee.

For too many years she'd watched her mother, who was always looking for "Mr. Right," turn to putty around any attractive man who flashed her a smile. Sam, on the other hand, was selective, preferring no man in her life instead of just anyone.

With her coffee cup in hand, she strolled into the sunroom and perched on the navy-and-burgundy-colored cushion of the window seat. If it hadn't been for her job and Max Montgomery's accident, she and Max would have never met, never been together now. She belonged to a world where people worked to meet bills. For leisure, she enjoyed a night at the movies or bowling or dinner at Sallie's BBQ in Big Timber, things that wouldn't break her budget. His world—well, this was it—crystal, antiques, expensive paintings.

Upstairs, Max drank the juice she'd brought him then, cradling the coffee cup in his hand, strolled toward a bookcase. For the life of him he couldn't remember reading any of these books.

On the wall behind the headboard was an abstract in various hues of blues and deep purple and splashes of black. Had he chosen it or was it another touch of an interior decorator?

In passing, he flicked on the CD player to hear what

music he'd chosen. The classical piece lulled and pleased him, but again sparked no memory.

His stomach knotted as he wrestled with a renewed sense of panic. What if he never mentally returned to the life he'd known? Who would he be? Could he go back to the bank? Could he resume relationships with family and friends even though no one's face was familiar?

Hell. He had to stop this. In an agitated move, he set the empty coffee cup on the tray and headed for the stairs. Eventually he would remember everything. The doctor had told him that the amnesia was temporary. Sometimes the mind needed a vacation when it was troubled too much. But what, he wondered, was bothering him?

In the hall, he slowed his stride and opened the door to the guest room Samantha had chosen. In one night she'd made herself at home. On the bedside table was an opened book. Bottles of brownish-red nail polish occupied a spot beside a hairbrush and a blow dryer, and nearby was a portable CD player. He couldn't help smiling. Though a suitcase full of clothes remained unpacked, she'd picked some yellow and white flowers from the garden and had found a vase.

He took only a few steps inside. She had a right to her privacy, but curious about the book she'd been reading, he ambled closer to read the title. It was an old best-seller written by an ex-president. An interesting choice.

Turning to leave, he spotted a lacy chemise in a

deep plum-color dangling out of the suitcase. A wispy piece of nothing made to send some poor sap crazy. Like him, he mused.

The image of that purple number stuck in his mind as he descended the stairs. He'd thought she'd be hustling around the kitchen. Instead he found her sitting on a cushioned window seat in the sunroom, sipping coffee. She looked ethereal, the crown of her red hair catching the light, a long shadow slanting across her face. It was, he realized, the first time he'd seen her so still.

He knew he hadn't moved. He'd barely breathed while staring at her. But as if he'd said something, she slowly angled a look his way. And she smiled. "I'll get your breakfast."

Max wanted to protest, to tell her not to move, but she whisked past him and toward the kitchen. He followed, reached it in time to watch her pour whipped eggs into a frying pan.

"I found a package of raspberries in the freezer." She stretched behind her to switch off the radio. "One of your cooks must have been a fruit lover and did a lot of freezing."

"Helga." Just like that, the woman's name had popped into his head. Max grabbed a kitchen chair, swung it around and straddled it. "Weird," he muttered with a shake of his head. "I can't remember people I've known all my life, but I remember her."

"What about her?"

"She stood eye-to-eye with me and could have been

a linebacker for the Seattle Seahawks." He scowled at the trivial information that filtered through while memories of his family eluded him.

Sam had watched his eyes glaze. "Do you remember more?"

"Why? Are you going to take notes?"

The sarcasm was unexpected. "Notes? Why would I?"

"Isn't your job to report back to someone?"

What he was talking about struck her. "I don't play spy well." Stiffening her back, she set down the spatula and faced him. "I have one job. To care for you. And if I answer to anyone, it's you. Although, out of courtesy since Rachel did hire me, if she asks me a question, I'll answer her honestly."

"You're something when you get going, aren't you?"

Sam ignored his comment. "Your breakfast is almost ready." While she would be responsible for reporting his physical progress, what memories came back to him really were his business. She did a quick count to three. Staying angry at anyone had never been her way. No longer miffed, she pivoted and held a spoonful of the fruity sauce out to him. "Taste. Tell me if I need to add more sugar to the raspberries." As she brought the spoon close to his lips, his eyes were on her, studying her. To her credit, she held the spoon steady for him. "Well?"

"Not bad."

"In other words, it's good." Funny that no one had told

her he was a tease. Or was it a rarely seen trait? She
returned to the counter and finished stirring the raspberries. "I'll keep you in mind for more of these kinds of
jobs." She flipped the omelet just as the toast popped.
Quickly she buttered it, then slid the omelet onto a plate.
For herself, she'd made toast only. "So what happened
to Helga?" Carrying the plates, she led the way to the
patio.

"She quit. She went back to Sweden."

Sam set his plate in front of him, then took a nearby
chair. "Did you send her running from the house in tears?"

"I doubt that." He took a hearty bite of the omelet.

"Is it okay?"

"Hmm," he said stingily.

Actions spoke louder than words. He was eating
the omelet with gusto.

"From what I remember about Helga, she'd lay me
flat with a frying pan before she'd burst into tears."

Sam watched the breeze ruffle his dark hair. "My
kind of lady."

Max would have guessed that. During the short time
he'd spent with her, he'd gotten a definite impression
that she stood tough when necessary.

"I need to go to the grocery store after breakfast.
Want to go with me?"

"Doesn't sound like something I'd do. But I'll give
you money for the groceries." He gestured with his fork
toward his plate. "This is good. Thanks."

Questioningly, Sam tipped her head. "Are you all
right?"

"What?"

"Did you hit your head again?"

His eyes grew puzzled. "What the hell are you talking about?"

"I thought you fell out of bed this morning." She waved a dismissive hand in the air. "But never mind. I was wrong."

"Wrong about what?"

"For a moment there, you were nice."

"Funny." Head bent, he heard her laugh, a throaty, soft sound.

Long after breakfast was over and Max was alone, that sound lingered in his mind. While she went to the grocery store, he rambled from room to room, trying not to think about her. He looked for a distraction, but he had no idea what to do with his free time and wished now that he'd gone with her. A trip to the grocery store had to be better than being alone.

He started reading a book about Custer's final confrontation at Little Bighorn. With boredom setting in, he was glad to hear Ellis's booming voice.

"Where are you, Max?" he yelled from the foyer. Lumbering into the living room where Max had finally relaxed with the book half an hour ago, Ellis went straight to the coffee tray Sam had left. "It's good to see you're up and around. Thought you might need some company." He swiveled a look over his shoulder. "Where's the nurse?"

"Grocery store."

"She doesn't know her place," he commented as if Max had asked his opinion about her.

Max averted his eyes and veiled a grin at the hint of admiration in Ellis's voice.

Ellis breezed on in a manner that meant he'd had his say; subject closed. "Did you remember more?"

No beating around the bush. Max realized he was still having trouble calling him dad. Did he call him that? Or father? Or was he Ellis to him? "Some oddball things."

Eyes like his own zeroed in on him. "Being here must help," his father said.

Actually Max had been more confused since coming home. He'd browsed through rooms, hoping some moment from the past of his being there would flash back at him. None did. He'd walked outside and stared at the tennis court. He wasn't even sure he played the game.

"You should go to the bank," Ellis advised. "You might remember something there."

"Bank business has been your world," Ellis had said to him when he'd been in the hospital. Max had wondered if anything else had mattered to him. Now he asked, "What did I do before taking the position as bank president?"

"I told you." Ellis lifted the carafe of coffee on the tray. "You traveled the country, overseeing my investments."

"Until when?" Max asked, watching his father pour himself coffee.

"About four years ago." Ellis stopped stirring the

sugar in his coffee. "I decided to run for mayor, so you settled back in Whitehorn and became the bank's president."

"Did I want to?"

"Want to?" Ellis scowled at Max as if he'd grown two heads. "Well, you needed to come here."

Because he'd wanted him to? Max wondered. "Where do you live?"

"At the house in town." His father's bushy brows veed as he raked a hand through his dark hair. "You grew up there."

Possibly if he saw it, he would remember. Max perched on the edge of a windowsill. "Do I ride?"

Ellis had caught his reflection in a window. "Ride what?" he asked, distracted, preening.

Max waited until his father tired of staring at his image. "A horse." Montana was horse country, wasn't it?

"Why, sure you can." Seeming unaware of his primping, he faced Max with renewed interest while he drank his coffee. "You don't have any of your own. You always said you were too busy."

"Working?"

"That's right." Ellis squinted at his wristwatch. "I'm supposed to see Kate after I leave here. She's still giving me trouble."

Max had no idea who he was talking about. "Kate?"

"Kate Randall Walker." Something akin to exasperation settled on his face. Max figured it was a pain to have to explain everything to someone.

"She's been a mighty fine judge. I'd consider a ticket with Montgomery and Walker a shoe-in. She'd be a terrific attorney general. But she keeps refusing."

"Why won't she run?"

"She says she's not the type. That's ludicrous. She has an impeccable reputation." With barely a breath taken, he shifted conversation again. "I told you what Garrett's doing, didn't I? He's going to have nothing but trouble if you ask me."

Max didn't bother to tell him that he didn't know anyone named Garrett.

"But he looks for it. Who else would go hunting for six grandsons, maybe seven? Illegitimate ones," Ellis was quick to add. "Only Garrett Kincaid. All of his grandsons were fathered by his late son Larry, who was a regular skirt-chaser. Anyway, Garrett is gung ho about buying the Kincaid ranch for them. But Jordan Baxter will fight him until hell freezes over."

Max's head spun. He didn't know the people that Ellis was talking about. "Why would this Baxter guy block the sale of the ranch?"

Ellis looked strangely at him for a second, only a second. "I'm sorry. I keep forgetting that you haven't sorted all of this out yet. Well, see, Jordan Baxter insists that the land is his. He produced a letter from his uncle Cameron that offered Jordan the right of first refusal to any sale. So Garrett can't do what he wants."

Finished with his coffee, he set down the cup. "Which is to divide the ranch as an inheritance for all those grandsons," he finished.

Max really didn't care. He managed to nod at the right moments as Ellis passed more inconsequential conversation with him, but he was growing tired of the constant stream of names and was ready for Ellis to leave.

"Guess I'll be going," he finally said, and checked his wristwatch once more. Max deduced that he'd scheduled so much time for his stay. Ellis stood, then started for the door but halted at the doorway. "Think about what I said. Go to the bank."

In the kitchen, Sam finished fluting a pie. When she'd returned from the grocery store, she'd seen Ellis Montgomery's car in the driveway. Now she heard his loud goodbye and craned her neck to look out the kitchen window to see if he'd left.

"There you are."

In response to the voice behind her, Sam jumped and whipped around.

"Been looking for you, missy. What's going on? What are you doing?"

Sam was baffled. What was Ellis accusing her of? He couldn't possibly know that she was mentally lusting for his son.

"I'm not pleased, missy."

Sam wiped her floured hands on a towel. "Excuse me?"

"He's not any better."

Sometimes the patient's family had the most difficult time accepting the circumstances of a loved one's illness. "He just got home, Mr. Montgomery. It takes time."

"How much time?" Ellis bellowed. "When is he going to get his head on straight?"

In the foyer, Max heard Ellis's shout. Was he worried about him because he was his son? Or was this about having a son not quite all right in the head? That could cause him some awkward moments while on the campaign trail.

Max waited until he heard Ellis slam the door on his way out, then entered the kitchen. Standing at the table, Sam was whipping something white and frothy. "What are you doing?"

Startled again, she whirled around. "You're quiet," she said with a hand pressed to her chest.

"Sorry." Frightening her hadn't been his goal. "Sorry about him, too. You didn't deserve his tirade."

"He's an upset father."

That she made an excuse for Ellis didn't surprise him. He sensed she had a gentle soul, a kind heart. "Ellis—my father." He paused again. "I have a hard time with that. I don't know him."

"Only do what you're comfortable with," she suggested as she spread the meringue on top of the lemon pie.

"We played catch-up about what I used to do." Max stood near the kitchen door and watched a jackrabbit scurry from one sagebrush to another. "It sounds familiar. Does that make sense? I can't remember my own father or my sister, yet I can remember bank business?"

"It's easier for you to remember."

"What the hell does that mean?"

Sam guessed where his indignation was coming from. He thought she was accusing him of not trying to remember more. She didn't bother to soothe him. He needed to face a few facts. "You don't want to remember more personal memories," she said bluntly. "At least, not yet."

"Is that what you've been told by a shrink?"

"What I was told came from the neurologist. Both doctors said that everyone should let you find your own way back."

What if he never did? Doubts never were far away, he realized.

"When Ellis talked to you about your work, did he mention Edna?"

"My assistant?" She'd come to visit him at the hospital. A pleasant woman in her late fifties, she seemed truly concerned for him. "I thought I'd call her tomorrow morning. I'll get back to work, even if it's at home."

She nodded as if that was a good idea. "You'd have time to call before we eat."

"Then, I will." Max stepped near and peered over her shoulder. "Lemon meringue pie. Do I like that?"

A smile lit her face. "It's on the list Rachel gave me. It's one of your favorites."

He'd like to see that list. It would make his life easier if he could simply read what he'd liked.

Four

Max had time for the phone call and a walk before dinner. More hungry than he realized, he took only a short trek around the estate.

On his way to the kitchen, he noticed she'd rented videos, a romantic comedy and an action-adventure movie. He thought he'd prefer the one that promised "death-defying stunts."

"Everything's ready," Sam announced when he joined her.

Dinner was as delicious as was everything she cooked. "What is this?" Max asked before popping another piece of meat into his mouth.

"It's pepper steak. It wasn't on the list, but I remember how wonderful this recipe was when I had dinner at Jessica and Sterling McCallum's."

Should he know them? Was he friends with them? "Friends who live in Whitehorn?" he asked.

"Yes. Almost from day one. Well, you know how Jessica is."

Actually he didn't.

"Oh." She bit her lip. For the first time since they'd met, she looked distressed. "I'm sorry. This must be difficult for you. And saying that to you was really insensitive."

Max wanted to ease her discomfort. "I don't know them, do I?"

"I couldn't say. I don't think so." She took empty salad plates to the sink. "But Jessica is naturally friendly and caring, so she makes friends easily. She's head of the social welfare department. Her husband is a special investigator in the sheriff's department," she rambled before returning to the table. "She's so good-hearted. Everyone likes her."

He merely nodded, more interested in the sight of the sunlight shimmering on her hair. "If she's such a great friend, she'd have talked you out of this job." He dug into his dinner again to stop his preoccupation with her, with the way she looked, with the way she made him feel. "Carter, why don't you leave?"

"Because you need me," she answered with a laugh.

Damn it, he really liked that sound. Dumb thinking, he supposed. But besides her being a knockout, whenever she came near, he caught a whiff of her scent, a fragile scent, one he couldn't forget even after she'd moved away. Disgusted with himself, he finished the meal in silence. He had no business thinking about her, about any woman, right now. With the last bite in his mouth, he pushed back his chair.

"I got videos for tonight, if you're interested."

"I'll think about it."

Bewilderment swept through Sam as she stared after him. Why the abrupt departure? Conversation had been civil, then he'd become quiet again.

Grabbing the plates, she moved to the sink to wash dishes. Perhaps it was best to leave him alone for a while. Later she would offer him the pie and coffee.

Sam watched the videos alone. Max had closeted himself in his room, and she spent a quiet evening by herself. With no company or conversation for hours, she welcomed the noise of others the next morning.

Before she eased out of the bed, her surroundings came alive with activity, the droning of an engine awakening her. At the bedroom window, she looked down to see the gardener running the riding lawn mower in precise straight lines over the stretch of rolling green at the back of the house.

Curious to meet him, Sam dressed then hurried down the steps.

She was on her way to the back door when the phone rang. Now that she was working at Max Montgomery's everyone she knew had questions. Yesterday Lily Mae Wheeler, the town busybody, had called to ask if the house was as beautiful as she'd heard.

This phone call was from Jessica. "I was checking to see if you're doing all right."

"I'm fine. He's fine. He had company. His father came by yesterday."

"That's a surprise."

Sam had heard talk about the Montgomerys. According to gossip, the politically ambitious Ellis had never paid Max or his sisters much mind. "Was there really no closeness between Ellis and his children?"

"Not really."

"What about his wife?" More than curiosity made Sam ask the question. She wondered if a lack of affection had made Max so distant. After all, Rachel came from the same family and she seemed warm and friendly. And Christina had been known for seeking attention anywhere she could find it. "Were they more of a family when Ellis's wife was alive?"

"Not really. Deidre Holworth wasn't Ms. Warmth. She was a refined woman from a socially prominent Montana family. She cared about appearances, about pedigrees."

"But weren't their lives different with her around?"

"They were never a loving family," Jessica assured her. "Before Max's accident, I think the last time the Montgomerys were together was for a family photo needed for Ellis's campaign. And Rachel didn't live here then. So they rarely spent time together."

Despite what Sam had lacked while growing up, she'd always known her mother loved her.

"I'll have to cut this short, Sam," Jessica said. "Sterling and Jenny want to go for a walk," she said about her husband and daughter. "But before I go, Sam, please remember that—well, you don't have to finish this."

"Of course, I do."

"If he's too impossible—"

Sam laughed. "Honestly, Jess, he's not so bad. I think his reputation as an ogre is exaggerated."

"Maybe that's true. And in fairness to him, a rich man doesn't understand problems of ordinary people. But he has a reputation as unfeeling and detached. I've heard stories repeatedly that he won't give extensions on loan notes, wouldn't authorize loans unless a person had collateral. That's his reputation."

"That's good business sense," Sam said in his defense.

"This is a small town. He's known a lot of these people all his life. He knows their character. That should count for something. He knows who's honest and hardworking. But he's Mr. Heart of Steel."

That might have been the man he'd been, but she was seeing a different man. A touch ornery, but certainly not ruthless.

Jessica continued, "And last month he fired the Crommer girl."

Samantha guessed Jessica was feeling compelled to relay gossip. "Who's she?" Samantha asked her.

"Jackson Crommer's daughter. The girl's mother was a school friend of Deidre's. The Montgomerys knew all of the Crommers. That didn't matter." Jessica clarified, "Of course, as bank president he had every right to fire her if she wasn't doing the job, but my point is that he has no soft spot."

Sam wondered if that was really true. She said goodbye to Jessica and set down the receiver. The sound of the lawn mower reminded her of her original goal to meet the gardener.

Showing no hesitation, he offered a bright greeting when she approached him minutes later. He then explained that the housekeeper, the one who'd run off in tears, was willing to come back, thanks to Rachel's call. A dozen questions and fifteen minutes later, Sam reentered the house.

There was no delicate way to discuss the problem with Max. Sam waited until he finished eating the pancakes she'd made for breakfast. With the soothing strains of a Beethoven concerto wafting on the air from the radio, she told him, "The housekeeper would be willing to come back and clean if—" Deliberately she paused to make sure she had his attention.

Over the rim of his coffee cup, he peered at her. "Come back?"

"She was your housekeeper until the day before the accident."

A frown bunched his dark brows. "Why did she leave?"

"You learned that she was seeing the gardener, and fired him."

More puzzlement darkened his eyes. "Wait a minute. Let me get this straight. I fired him but she left?"

"She didn't want him fired, so she chose to quit." Sam stretched behind her for the sugar bowl on the counter. "Now she'll come back if—"

"If what?"

She couldn't soften the explanation. "If she answers to me, not you."

He winced.

"Should I tell her no?"

"No. You weren't hired to clean this museum. Hire her back."

"I'll call Rachel and tell her what you decided."

He returned his attention to the pancakes. "What day off did my sister give you?"

"She didn't." Sam spooned sugar into her coffee. "We both assumed you'd make that decision."

"What day would you like?"

She'd given that part of her job no consideration. Off the top of her head, she thought she'd like Thursdays off. Usually there was a telecast of a baseball game on Thursday. She'd like to make popcorn and watch the game from beginning to end. "Tomorrow?"

"That's okay. You can go out. I don't need a—"

Sam interrupted. "I don't have to go out. What I want to do is here."

Curiosity flickered in his eyes. "What's that? Swim? Play tennis?"

"Watch a baseball game."

"Baseball?" Why was he surprised? "If you want, watch it on the big screen in the den."

His offer pleased her. At home, she owned a television with a thirteen-inch screen. "Want to keep me company? Or don't you like baseball?"

"I like it. I played third base in college." He

appeared dumbfounded. "I'll be damned. Where did that come from?"

"What do you remember about playing?"

What did he remember? Max concentrated hard on the nearby wall, tried to visualize. He saw uniforms that were white with a gray stripe running down the sides of the legs. A white hat with a bluish-gray bill. He heard cheers, lots of cheers, and grinned with the memory. "Hitting a grand slam. Do you know what that is?"

"Who do you think you're talking to?" She cast a pseudo affronted look his way. "I became a real baseball fan when we lived near Houston."

"Why?"

"Joe lived for the game."

"Joe was a boyfriend?"

"Stepfather."

"You had a good relationship with him, then."

"With all of them." She hummed a few notes with the music that was drifting on the air. "Don't you love this concerto?"

His gaze shifted from the radio to her. "What's with the highbrow music? I thought you liked blues."

"I love Beethoven, too. Ian gave me that. He was a musician who played electric guitar with a group at local clubs, but he loved all music. When I was nine, he introduced me to Beethoven's 'Moonlight Sonata.' From that moment on, I was hooked."

"Ian was…?"

"Another stepfather."

How many were there? Max wondered. "So you

like Beethoven and baseball. What else? Skydiving?
Hang gliding?"

Sam realized he was actually teasing her again.
"Nothing so exciting, though I'd like to hang glide
sometime. But I do have a brown belt in karate."

"No, you don't." As she laughed, Max accepted the
obvious. This woman was far from ordinary. Baseball,
Beethoven and a brown belt. There were a lot of layers
here. He'd like to peel them back one-by-one and
discover everything about her.

"Do you want to watch the game?" she asked. "I'll
bring the popcorn. You bring—"

"The beer."

"Works for me." This definitely was not the man
people kept warning her about. At a distinctive sound
from outside, Sam looked out the window and saw the
postal carrier truck. "Mail's here. I'll go get it."

She was a step from the door when he called out,
"Hey, Carter."

Samantha grasped the doorknob, but didn't turn it,
and shifted her stance toward him. "What?"

"Can you make *chile rellenos* stuffed with
chicken?"

"Can I?" Who'd have expected such a question?
"Hot enough to make smoke come out of your ears, Mr.
Montgomery."

"It's Max."

She'd heard him, but asked, "What?"

"Call me Max."

Suddenly she was on a first-name basis with him.

A smart woman would have viewed that step forward as a giant warning. Not her. Showing traces of being her mother's daughter, she couldn't think of anything but the fact that she suddenly felt warm and fuzzy just because he'd smiled at her.

Nothing was in sync in his world. Max couldn't get a handle on the man who lived in this mausoleum. Why would he have such a big place just for himself? And what did he do when he was home? There was a tennis court and a heated swimming pool. Whom did he play tennis with? Did he swim daily? Who came over to play billiards with him? Why weren't the pieces of the puzzle called his life falling into place?

And why was he letting one woman inch her way under his skin? She wasn't a part of the world he was trying to recapture. She'd only complicate his life.

Trying to get some direction as to his daily routine, he called the bank after dinner to talk to his assistant again. "Edna, it's Max," he said when the woman answered the phone.

"Mr. Montgomery?"

"Edna, would you come over Thursday instead of Friday with whatever is current on my desk?"

"Yes, sir. What time?"

"Three or four. Whatever works for you."

Bafflement colored her voice. "Whatever works for— Yes, sir."

"Okay. See you then, Edna."

"Yes, sir."

Max placed the phone on its base. How long had the woman worked for him? From what Ellis had said she'd been at the bank a long time, but he gathered no closeness existed between them. Why not?

Damn it, he was tired of all the questions.

There had to be something in the house that clicked his memory. From the foyer, he wandered into the den. The room was masculine, done in dark woods. He noticed that a plant he'd thought needed to be tossed was showing new life. In passing, he dabbed a finger into the soil. It was moist, no doubt the recipient of Carter's TLC.

He'd noticed, too, that most of the bookshelves contained biographies and nonfiction. He kept looking and finally spotted a mystery and a few thrillers among them. Could amnesia change a man so he had different likes and dislikes?

With a shift of his body, he was staring at a photograph on the desk. Ellis sat in a chair like a king on the throne. On one side of him, Max stood, unsmiling. To the other side of the old man were his daughters. The taller, Rachel, with her shoulder-length dark hair and dark blue eyes, had a quieter beauty than their younger sister. Christina, petite and curvy, with a dimpled smile, was a pouty-faced beauty.

He stared hard at her, so hard his eyes hurt, but he couldn't remember her. Had they been close as kids? What about him and Rachel? Questions. Always so damn many questions. Swearing, he spun around to find Samantha standing in the doorway.

"I didn't mean to bother you," she said.

That was impossible. She bothered him constantly.

"I came in to—well, could I borrow a book?"

Nothing was easy. He felt strange that she had to ask him a question like that. Everything around him was his, he reminded himself. The problem was, he didn't remember any of it. "You're free to use whatever you want. The swimming pool, the tennis court, the books. Whatever."

"Thank you." In the past, Sam had several patients who'd given her the same permission, but she hadn't been sure about Max. Crossing the room toward the bookshelves, she again saw a distant look in his eyes, as if he were in a trance. "Max?"

He blinked. "I don't remember her," he said, sharing the one thought he couldn't get out of his head. He rounded a look at her. "Did you know Christina?"

"No, I didn't. Do you know that she—"

He guessed the reason for her hesitation. "Died?" he finished for her. "Yes. Ellis told me when I was in the hospital. What exactly happened?"

"Didn't he tell you?"

"Not details. I know she was killed."

"She disappeared last August."

"Just like that. She was here one day, then gone?"

Sam bridged the space between them. "Kate Randall Walker—do you know who she is?"

Max leaned his backside against the edge of the desk. "A judge. Ellis wants her to run on the ticket with him."

"Kate was at the Hip Hop on the last day Christina was seen. She said that Christina was on the phone and looked distraught."

"Who was she calling?"

Sam had heard it all. The gossipers had had a field day when Christina first disappeared. Anything that had to do with the Montgomerys was newsworthy. "When they began tracing Christina's actions, you told the authorities that she'd called you."

"And I went to see her?"

"No, you didn't."

She watched tension take over.

His back straightened; his jaw tightened. "Why didn't I?" he asked.

"I don't know the answer to that."

"Tell me about her. What do you know?"

"Not a lot. She was outgoing, a bit of a flirt."

His eyes bored into hers. "What aren't you saying?"

"I only know what the gossips said." She observed his hand gripping the edge of the desk so tightly that his knuckles had whitened. "Everyone had thought Christina looked pregnant. And then she disappeared."

"Who was the father?"

"I don't know." Seeing his deepening frown, Sam thought she might have given him too much to think about. "Why don't we talk about this later."

"No," he snapped. "Now. Tell me what you know."

Sam had no choice. Steel-blue eyes trapped her. "Days passed, and since all her things were still in her room, authorities had to consider a kidnaping. They waited, but no ransom note came." Sam longed to stop, but she understood his need to learn everything, to piece together a puzzle. "Along with the help of local psychics Crystal Cobbs and her aunt, Winona Cobbs, Deputy Sloan Ravencrest found Christina's body after several months of searching. Everyone was convinced she'd had a baby before she died. Everyone also had doubts the baby would ever be found."

"Was it?"

Sam nodded. She was glad to give him some better information. "Rachel got the baby, rather anonymously. The baby was dropped off on her porch with a note from the father saying he would be back. At the time, Rachel suspected the baby was Christina's."

"Did she have it tested?"

"Yes, and a DNA test proved that the baby was Christina's."

Slowly he shook his head as if trying to make sense of everything she'd said. "What about the father?"

"No one knew who he was. And for a while, authorities believed that Emma Stover was guilty of the murder."

"Emma Stover." He considered the name for a long moment. "The name means nothing to me."

"She's a waitress at the Hip Hop. But she isn't the one who did it," Sam was quick to tell him. "Deputy Sloan Ravencrest and the sheriff declared that evidence—"

He held up a hand. "What kind?"

Meeting his steady, unflinching stare, Sam told him

what she'd heard. "Strands of hair, fiber, drops of blood that were not the victim's, and footprints from the scene cleared Emma. And it cleared Homer Gilmore."

"Another name." Disgust threaded his voice. "Another person I don't know. Who is he?"

"He's an eccentric old man. You'll see him around town once in a while."

"So the murderer hasn't been caught?" he said so softly she strained to hear him.

"No, Max. But I heard that the sheriff plans to test several men."

"Test?"

"DNA," Sam answered.

"Hell." He closed his eyes for only a second as if there was something too painful to look at. "I suppose I should feel something about her but I don't."

What she felt was his discomfort. Compassion flowed through her. How hard this all was for him. He could pretend to roll with each new piece of information, but there was such pain in his eyes. Jessica had said that he had no soft spot. That wasn't true, Sam thought. She'd seen his vulnerability at not being able to remember a sister who'd died. "Max—" As she reached out to touch his cheek, he stepped back. Sam didn't even try to get past the wall he'd so quickly erected.

"Let it go," he said in a tone that sounded more angry at himself than her. He heaved a deep breath and squinted at the mountains. "Where do you live?"

Sam assumed he was looking for a distraction from

his own troubled thoughts. "In a small apartment around the corner from the Hip Hop. It's a one bedroom, but it's all I need. I'm out of it more than in it."

"Is there a man waiting at home for you?"

Why would he ask that? It means nothing, she berated herself. He's making conversation. "We're supposed to be finding out about you, not me." Her voice trailed off as he reached out and toyed with a strand of hair near her ear. The touch was far lighter, far gentler, than she expected.

"You'd be more interesting."

Her eyes snapped up to meet his. Usually she loved the unexpected, spontaneity. But he'd caught her off balance. Never had she anticipated his making a move on her. Maybe he wasn't. Maybe she was making too much of his touch.

"There's no one, is there?" he asked in a low voice that sounded dangerous.

He curled his fingers around her arm, and as if in slow motion, he tugged her closer. She was imagining nothing, she realized now, standing between his legs. She should have pulled back, but she was curious. "I—" The token protest died when his mouth caressed first one corner of her lips and then the other.

He murmured something. She didn't care what he'd said. She wanted to dive into his kiss. Her heart pounding, when his lips met hers firmly, she slipped her hands around to his back and braced for sensation. It did no good. Excitement rushed through her.

Tongues met and dueled. Using only a kiss, he weakened her; he seduced her.

And her heart felt suddenly fragile. That frightened her. How often had her mother felt like this? Sam made herself remember. Wasn't this kind of feeling what she'd vowed to avoid?

As a slow-moving ache fluttered through her, she wavered between deepening the kiss or tearing her mouth from his. She knew the insanity of letting the moment go on. Still she didn't move away as his lips twisted against hers. She tried to tell herself the kiss was nice, nothing more. But her pulse pounded, and she felt hungry for more, far hungrier than she'd ever been.

Before the will to stop him was lost, breathless, she wedged a hand between them. How could she think of him objectively if he dissolved all her good sense, if she let him snatch the breath from her? "That was—" *Exciting.*

His hand slid down her arm as if he couldn't not touch. "What…what was it?" He sounded just as breathless.

Shaken, Sam barely managed to keep her voice steady. "A mistake." She might be just a convenience to him. Or he might have kissed her because he was confusing attraction with gratitude. Briefly, she hesitated, then turned away. She left the room with the warmth of his kiss still lingering on her lips.

Five

She was wrong. Max knew that hadn't been a mistake. While her softness had pressed against him during the kiss yesterday, he'd realized how much he needed her in ways that had nothing to do with sex. With a smile, a laugh, a kiss, she'd made him feel less angry about his own inadequacies, less vulnerable.

No one else had done that. When he'd been in the hospital, the doctors, nurses, his family, had all assured him that he'd get back his memory. Only he still had doubts. Even now, after coming home.

So now what? Did he forget the past and make new memories? Should he grab what was within his reach—his sister, father, his job—a redhead who made him smile, a woman whose kiss had leveled him?

He could have pushed for more, but he honestly

didn't like wanting her so much. It didn't matter that he needed her, that with his attraction to her he felt a sense of normalcy. He'd also felt as if control might slip away with one more sampling of her taste. And that, he realized, he didn't like. So he'd learned from a kiss, and from the desire heating his gut, that control mattered to him. He learned, too, it would slip easily around her.

Wearing jeans, he shrugged into a shirt, but it remained unbuttoned. After wiggling his feet into deck shoes, he left the bedroom. From the top of the stairs, he heard movement below. The slam of a door, the quickness of footsteps. He expected to see Sam when he reached the kitchen. He saw the housekeeper instead.

Around thirty-something with brown hair drawn back and held at the nape of the neck by a clip, Louise sent him a sheepish look that made Max mentally grimace. She was a sweet thing. Shy, Samantha had told him. And afraid of him, Max surmised. This wouldn't do, not at all. He looked for a way to break the ice between them. "That smells good," he said about the cake cooling on a rack.

Louise returned a token smile.

"I thought you only kept house?"

"I— Samantha said I could bake it during my break."

As her voice grew anxious, Max held up a hand. "Whoa. It's okay if you're in here. Whatever Samantha said is okay."

Her smile widened slightly. "Thank you, sir."

"Who's the cake for?"

"For Martin. For his birthday. I wanted to make a cake but wouldn't have had time when I got home."

Max delivered his best smile to relax her. "Is Martin a relative?"

"He's—" She pointed toward the window. Outside the gardener was pulling weeds from a flower bed. "Martin is the gardener."

Right. Now Max remembered Samantha telling him about their affair. Why had he opposed their relationship?

The thought troubled him. How heartless had he been? he wondered. He left Louise to ice the cake with chocolate frosting, and searched for Sam. Earlier this morning, from his bedroom window, he'd caught a glimpse of her jogging into the nearby woods. He couldn't say what had grabbed his attention more, the neon-green baseball cap or the snug fit of her jeans.

Stepping outside, he found her at the pool, looking like some sea nymph as she cut through the clear water with smooth, fluid strokes. She swam with the same kind of endless energy she used to move around the house. After a dozen laps, she lifted herself onto the cool deck and tossed back slick-looking hair. She was wearing a two-piece yellow suit that shifted his imagination into high gear. When she slanted a look his way, water streamed down her throat, caressed the flesh at the shadowed vee of her breasts. Sunlight played across her wet skin, shone on her hair. She made him think of mermaids.

"Hi. I thought I'd let you sleep." She stretched for a peach-colored terry robe on a nearby chaise longue. "Are you ready to shower now?"

"There's no hurry."

She wrapped herself in the robe. "Did you know you have a pool man?"

Max dropped onto one of the patio chairs. He realized they were going to pretend nothing had happened yesterday. For now, because he wasn't sure what direction he wanted to take in their relationship, he followed her lead. "I seem to have a truckload of servants. Like Louise." He eyed the thin, slightly balding man who'd finished weeding and was trimming a bush. "And Martin."

"There's José, too." She shook her wet hair away from her face. "He's the pool man. He comes once a week. And Gibson, your butler."

"Don't know him."

"You might remember him when he returns from his vacation. He'd taken a Caribbean cruise and is now visiting relatives in England. But if Mr. Montgomery needed him, he would return immediately." She grinned. "That's what he said. Rachel called him back and told him that a private nurse had been hired so he could finish out his vacation. And Foster, the chauffeur, returned, too. He lives in the apartment above the garage."

During a stroll around the property, Max had noticed the limo parked in the three-car garage. "What else did you learn about him?"

Her eyes narrowed. "Why do you think I did?"

"You did." He believed she would talk to a tree if no one was around.

"Are you casting aspersions about my gift for gab?"

Max barely held back a laugh at her quaint way of saying she prattled. "Well, did you learn more?"

"As a matter of fact, yes, I did. His name is Evan Foster. He retired from the military three years ago, then decided he needed to work. He'd been visiting friends in Seattle while you were in the hospital."

For a long moment Max studied her. He would like to forget anyone else existed. It suddenly occurred to him what the kiss had really done. No longer could he think of her as an employee. No longer was she just his nurse.

Hearing the quick click of heels behind him, he turned to see Louise. A man behind her showed impatience. Tall and slightly overweight, he had medium brown hair and a round face. Wearing an expensive suit and shoes, he stepped around Louise instead of waiting to be announced. "Hey, good buddy. Someone said you conked yourself good on the head."

Before he reached them, Sam was standing. "Excuse me. I need to change." She looked from Max to the man. "Enjoy your visit."

"Merv Talbot," he said, and turned on the charm. "You don't have to leave on my account." He offered her a hand. "You look familiar."

Max had no choice except to make the introduction. "Samantha Carter." He had no idea who Merv "Good

Buddy" Talbot was. But he didn't like the way Talbot watched her until she disappeared. Crazy or not, Max felt like taking a poke at him.

"She's familiar," Talbot said with more certainty.

"She's my private nurse. Been in town for five years."

"No. I've seen her somewhere else." He looked around him. "Isn't that cook here anymore? I could use a cup of coffee."

"She left," Max said, though unsure who Talbot was talking about.

"Never mind." He dropped to an adjacent chair and gave Max an assessing look. "I would have visited when you were in the hospital, but I've been handling commercial property in Bozeman."

"This isn't easy, but how do I know you?" Max finally asked.

"How do you— Oh, damn. I'm a Realtor." He beamed, widening his face. "*The* Realtor in town," he corrected, exhibiting no modesty. "We've been friends for years. I came to see if you were able to go on our fishing trip." He motioned toward Max's arm in the cast. "Guess not."

"Hardly," Max returned. "Where were we going?"

"Where were we— Oh, yeah. You don't remember, do you? We'd planned to spend a week in Deadman's Basin, catch some rainbow trout. You, me, and my brother-in-law Alan." His voice trailed off. "I remember now. I told you she looked familiar. You said her name was Carter? Nevich told me about her."

"Nevich?"

"Raymond Nevich is a lawyer in Big Timber. She was there caring for someone," he said, shifting conversation back to Samantha. "That's when Ray remembered her. He visited his sister who lived in Lubbock, Texas. Nevich said he remembered his sister telling him about her neighbors. His sister lived in a trailer court and next door was a woman and her daughter. Sammi was the daughter's name. The girl was a real looker. That she is." Talbot winked at Max. "She may be a nurse now, but she used to dance topless at some club. What was the name of it?" He paused, then snapped his fingers. "I remember. The Cottontail Club."

In the next breath, he rattled on about the great fishing Max would miss. Max could have cared less. He was glad to see Talbot leave. In fairness to him, Max excused his dislike of the man to his mood, and Talbot's tale about Sam.

It was rare for Sam to laze around even on her day off, but this morning an edgy mood nagged at her. Romance hadn't been part of her plans when she'd taken this job. She wasn't supposed to get involved with a patient. Oh, she'd heard of other private nurses who'd gone to a job and had found love. Only Sam had always viewed love like a brass ring—just out of her reach. She'd also concluded that the attraction between her and Max had nothing to do with love. Lust, most likely.

Still, a trace of Teresa Carter's little girl existed, the one who'd grown up around a woman so inclined toward fantasies of Prince Charming that the nightly bedtime story had been *Cinderella*. Sam doubted she'd ever free herself of the young girl who'd been raised on her mother's dream of forever love and happily-ever-after.

While she'd dressed, she'd debated about what to do next. She and Max had developed a routine of sorts. Though she assisted him with the buttons on his shirts and the ties on his shoes, he bathed himself now with the help of a long-handled shower brush.

Since Talbot's visit, Max had been quieter than usual. Sam had helped him dress, then left him alone. She couldn't make him tell her what was troubling him. But she was grateful he'd decided not to make an issue of the kiss. That suited her. It would be best if they both forgot about it.

At noon, she sought him out. On the patio, he appeared engrossed in a book. When Sam mentioned lunch, he said he wasn't hungry.

Sam frowned with concern for him, and strolled toward the kitchen. Perhaps they'd both been cooped up too long and needed to get out. But what should they do? Alone, she'd visit friends or go to a movie. What was his social life? Since he couldn't tell her, she had to rely on Rachel for answers.

The phone call to her wasn't enlightening.

"He works," Rachel said.

Sam couldn't believe that was all he did. "He has a

tennis court. Who did he play with?" Though he couldn't resume the sport, with Rachel's answer, she would at least learn the name of a friend.

"Max preferred handball. The previous owner had the tennis court."

"Rachel, I thought we'd visit friends or neighbors of his," she said to explain the reason for her questions.

"Good luck, Sam. I don't think he really knows his neighbors. He usually kept to himself."

Sam planned to change that. Socializing was good for the soul. People needed people. She laughed. That sounded like lyrics from an old Barbra Streisand song. But it was the truth.

With plans for time away from the house cemented in her mind, she joined Louise in the kitchen and made crab salad for lunch. She shared it with Louise and Martin, and when finished, they spent the rest of lunchtime playing gin rummy.

Leaving them just before one, Sam headed for the den and the big-screen TV to watch the baseball game. Though unsure, because of Max's mood, if he would join her for the game, she'd popped enough popcorn for both of them.

Max couldn't remember a word he'd read. He looked at letters and turned pages, but thoughts of a certain redhead had teased his mind. Because of Talbot, he'd grown more curious about her. Actually that was her fault. Because she tended to not talk about herself, he wanted to know more. But did he have a right? Plain and simple, her past was not his business. With that thought, he entered the den to join her for the baseball game.

"This player is a sucker for an inside pitch," she announced brightly when he neared the sectional sofa.

She looked adorable wearing a fielder's cap, a yellow T-shirt and skintight jeans that molded to her long, slender legs, making any man drool. Before he did, he zeroed in on the men on the playing field, and dropped to a cushion on the opposite end of the sofa. "You don't know what you're talking about." He accepted a bowl overflowing with popcorn from her and shoved a handful into his mouth. "He's their heavy hitter," he mumbled. "He smacked three homers in another game a few months ago."

"A memory came back?" Looking interested, she shifted toward him on the sofa cushion.

He couldn't be thrilled. "Hardly an earth-shattering one," he said with the disgust he felt over such trivial remembrances.

"Any one is important."

He disagreed but didn't argue.

"He's going to strike out," she predicted. With the pitcher's wind-up, she glued her eyes to the television screen. When the batter swung hard and missed, she groaned. "Told you. Did you see that? He's an easy out," she insisted, propping those incredible legs on the coffee table and crossing her bare feet at the ankles.

She was cute but wrong. Max snorted and dragged

his gaze from her. On the television screen, the batter dug his feet into the dirt, swung at a pitch and missed.

"Okay, make a bet," she challenged.

She was more entertaining than the baseball game, he decided. "What bet?"

"If I'm right, you do what I want to do." She glanced back at the television. "Come on." She rushed him for an answer before the next pitch. "Yes or no?"

"What do I get?" he asked, not about to be hurried.

Sam didn't miss the devilish glint in his eyes. "Watch," she said rather smugly. The pitcher wound up, took a long stride forward and released the ball. It spun hard, and as it crossed the plate, it curved. The batter practically drilled himself into the ground for a third out. "Told you. He's out."

He was impressed. "Okay, how did you know that?"

Her eyes sparkling, she appeared tempted to gloat. "He's been in a slump for the past month. He has the highest statistic for strike-outs on his team."

"How could I know that? I've been in the hospital."

"You had a television."

"I didn't watch it," he came back quickly. "You should forfeit."

Sam laughed. "Sore loser."

No, he hadn't been a loser. He'd enjoyed the afternoon with her. Later, while sitting alone, he couldn't deny he felt different, unbelievably good-humored, as if all was right in the world when he was with her. Crazy thinking. He honestly hadn't thought he wanted to know her better. What was the point in having feelings for a woman who wasn't supposed to be part of his life?

With the sound of footsteps on the gleaming foyer floor, he brought himself back to his surroundings. Since Louise, the housekeeper, plodded with heavier steps, he ambled to the doorway to see where Samantha was going.

Sunglasses on, she lugged a half-filled bucket of soapy water toward the door.

"What are you planning now?" Max asked before she reached the door.

Startled, she jerked to a stop and whipped around. Her eyes darted to the bucket and the sloshing water. "You nearly scared me to death." With the back of her hand, she brushed away strands of hair not tucked under the green baseball cap. "My heart's still in my throat." She eyed the bucket again. "I was planning to wash my car."

"It needs more than a wash." He hadn't been impressed with the dark blue, four-wheel-drive vehicle. Some rust had begun at the rocker panels.

In a regal manner, she nudged the sunglasses to the bridge of her nose and peered over the rim at him. "It's more dependable than some people. It got me through a blizzard to reach a woman in labor," she told him. "And it made the trip down a back road so I could join a rescue team after a flood." Obviously not as offended as she'd seemed, she laughed. "Though it was a jostling ride over some of the deepest ruts I've ever seen. And it even hauled a brand-new heifer to the vet's for a neighbor boy."

Max stared at her in amazement. What she didn't say mattered more. She'd weathered that blizzard and the flood to help others. She'd shown compassion and caring for a boy worrying about his farm animal.

"It's really looking dirty since the last rain." She squinted toward the window. "What time is Edna coming?"

He'd forgotten. "Soon."

"Well, enjoy your visit," she said, starting toward the door.

He wandered into the living room and stilled beside the piano. Out the window, he watched her slop a large, soapy sponge across the hood of the car. When she bent forward across it, he was left with a maddening but delectable view of her trim, tight backside in the snug jeans.

Questions again plagued him. She had the body for exotic dancing. With that bubbly personality, she belonged in a hub of excitement, should have been a dancer or a cocktail waitress or a casino dealer.

A dancer. Had she been one? He swore at himself and ended his preoccupation with her, especially that cute little backside, before he drove himself crazy. Scanning the keyboard, he placed a finger on a key. "Middle C." He touched another. "B flat." Caught up in the sounds, he let his fingers dance over more keys. A melody developed. Something sultry and soft called "Deep Purple."

Pleasure skimming through him, he smiled with the personal enjoyment and the new knowledge that he could play the piano and liked rhythm and blues.

"Pretty." Sam's voice made him look up. "Edna is here," she called from the doorway. "I'll be upstairs. I need to shower."

She whirled away to let Edna step inside.

"Good afternoon, Mr. Montgomery."

Max eyed the stack of manila folders in her arms.

"As you requested, I brought the foreclosures you'd been working on before the accident."

"All of those?"

"These have mortgages that haven't been paid in five or six months." She lifted one folder. "The day of the accident you had an appointment with Dwayne Melrose."

Power. There was a lot of power in his job. He could destroy lives, take away homes. "Edna, please sit down." He gestured to a wing-armed, brown leather chair beside the desk. While she took a seat and set the folders on his desk, he settled on the chair behind it. "Because of the amnesia, you're going to have to help me. Who is Dwayne Melrose? Tell me about him."

Briefly puzzlement knitted her brows. If she had questions, she didn't ask them. "Dwayne's a third gen-eration rancher. The land was passed down from his grandfather to his father to him."

"Not exactly a fly-by-night type."

A slim smile widened her face. "Dwayne Melrose, and his wife Emily are church-going, civic-minded people. If someone needs help with a barn-raising or a fund-raiser, Dwayne, his wife and kids are there."

"Then what happened that he didn't make payments?"

"Dwayne got sick. His boys, Craig and Larry, came to help after they were done with their work shifts, but without someone to do the work full-time—well…"

Max raised a hand to stop her. "I get the idea. Will an extension help them?"

A softness entered her hazel eyes. "Of course, it would. Emily, his wife, told me that they planned to sell livestock. They would do anything to hold on to their ranch."

Max tapped a pencil on his desk. "Okay."

She looked perplexed. "Sir?"

"Give him the extension."

"Give him— Oh, sir!" She glowed with a pleasure that deepened every line in her face. "I'll notify Dwayne and Emily today, sir."

Max winced at her formality. This had to stop. "Look, Edna, I don't know what I was like before, but why don't we pretend—"

"Pretend?" Her eyes widened.

Max guessed he wasn't prone to such impractical behavior. He went on anyway. "Pretend," he repeated, "that we're starting over, and don't call me sir."

She looked unconvinced but agreed. "If you'd prefer that."

"I'd really prefer that," he assured her. "Now, would you like coffee or something?"

"Sir?" She released a soft, amused laugh. "It will take time to remember not to call you that."

"I never offered coffee before, did I?" Max asked, sensing the reason for her confusion.

"No, I've never even been here."

She'd never been to his house before? He doubted many people had. Looking at the grand surroundings, he noticed Samantha standing in the doorway. No doubt she'd heard Edna. Was she wondering what kind of man he'd been? She related well to everyone she met. Obviously he didn't.

Earlier he'd seen her playing gin rummy in the kitchen with Louise and Martin. After years of employing them, he hadn't even known their names, yet she'd met them only a day ago and was socializing with them. Hell! Was he being too hard on himself? He probably knew their names, but because of the amnesia, he couldn't remember them. But what about Edna? Why had he never tried to have a better relationship with her?

Max drew his errant thoughts back to work and once again focused on the details Edna imparted. He didn't remember some of the cases they discussed, and struggled to keep up with her. He assured himself that with time all that he'd forgotten would return.

When Edna stood to leave, Max rose, too. "Thank you for coming, Edna," he said as he saw her to the door. As soon as he shut it behind his assistant, Sam appeared in the hallway.

"Let's go out," she declared. As his frown started to

form, she added in a cajoling voice, "For a ride, Max. We both need to get out."

"It was your idea to stay home and watch the ball game," he reminded her. "If you'd wanted to go out, you should have gone."

By yourself was unsaid but heard. Samantha slanted a grin at him. "You're a sore loser. You promised to do what I wanted if I won." None too graciously, she reminded him. "I won. So come on."

"There's nowhere I want to go." The memory of her bending across her car lingered. He took a breath to ease his annoyance. No such luck. She'd moved near. With her sudden closeness, her scent, a delicate flowery fragrance, assailed his senses.

"It'll just be a ride. I'll meet you at the car. I have to get something."

"Whatever," he murmured. Actually he grumbled.

Six

Before he thought of an excuse not to go, Sam hurried to the kitchen to pack a picnic basket. Earlier when the plan had taken hold, she'd prepared food.

She kept telling herself this was about his well-being. She was only doing her job, but she rarely lied to herself. This was about the heat he'd stoked during that kiss. She wanted to get to know him better on a level that had nothing to do with her being his nurse.

Not wise, she supposed. Anyone could see how different they were. He relied on intelligence and reasoning, on sensibility. His life had revolved around numbers, money, the bottom line. She let emotions lead her, focused on people.

She doubted he would ever understand her. And maybe she wouldn't understand him, either, the man he'd been. But then, this wasn't about that man. This, whatever this was that she felt for him, was about the man he was right now.

She felt his vulnerability, and his strength. It couldn't be easy to face a mirror and not recognize the person in it. But he exhibited such determination about finding that man again.

And while she admired him, and he'd endured her, oddly a compatibility of sorts had developed.

With Louise and Martin and the birthday cake gone, Sam had the kitchen to herself. It took only minutes to pack the picnic basket.

She rushed to the car, glancing at the heavy pewter clouds as she placed the picnic basket in the back seat, then joined Max who was already in the car. He never looked her way even when she hooked his seat belt. Eyes closed, head back, he seemed intent to prove he wasn't going happily along. Why was he so annoyed with her? She'd done nothing.

With the engine running, the radio on, and Al Hirt wailing out "Harlem Nocturne" on his trumpet, Sam hummed along while she enjoyed the drive. If Max didn't want to talk, so be it. Contrary to what he might believe, she could be quiet, and set out to prove that.

She was bothering him—a lot. It had taken a moment for Max to key in on why he felt uneasy. It was her quietness. It wasn't natural for her to be so quiet. Sitting beside him, she'd said nothing since they'd left the house, just hummed.

Eyes still closed, he let the soft, sultry sound swirl around him. He felt the warm breeze on his face, caught the smell of rain drifting on the air. Easily he imagined the wind lifting the fiery strands of her hair and tossing them away from her face. Damn. This was why he'd resisted a cozy afternoon of one-on-one with her. Without doing anything, she could bewitch a man.

"Here we are."

Her brightly said announcement coincided with an abrupt, jarring stop. When the sound of the engine died, Max snapped open his eyes. The slam of a car door followed. She was on the move, rounding the front of the car.

"It's really beautiful."

His heart lurched. No, she was. A hint of sunlight caressed her face, shadowing its delicate features. The wind ruffled her hair, plastered her blouse against her breasts. And his resistance dissolved.

"It's so open. So endless," she continued.

Where they were was in the middle of nowhere. "What are we doing here?"

"We're going to have a picnic."

Food. In a basket? Sliding out of the car, Max cast a glance at the prairie grass. Over his shoulder, he saw her lifting the basket from the car. "What's in there? Peanut butter and jelly sandwiches?"

"You're deliberately being difficult again, aren't you?"

He supposed he was. "Could be."

"A picnic will be fun." She tucked a blue plaid

blanket under her arm and flashed a sunshiny smile at him.

Guilt fluttered through him. He shouldn't give her such a hard time, but it was that or total surrender. She'd have him on his knees if he wasn't careful.

"You'll see. Come on," she urged, even as she stopped. "Aha." She stood in place and scanned her surroundings. "There. That's perfect."

Max guessed that protesting would be futile. She was fanning the blanket under a giant cottonwood. "What are we eating?"

"Shrimp salad. Breast of chicken. I think you'll like everything." As he joined her on the blanket, she shifted to set a small picnic basket between them. "I brought fruit salad, too."

Max braced his back against the tree trunk.

In the distance, storm clouds gathered above the Crazy Mountains.

"Did you have a good visit with your friend?"

"He says he's one. I'm not sure." With the mention of Talbot, she'd opened the door to his curiosity. "Before nursing, what kind of jobs did you have?"

"Jobs?" She looked up from the basket. "Where did that come from?"

"It's small talk, Sam." She moved, leaned closer. Temptation hummed through him to touch her. "Tell me who you are."

She laughed airily. "A fortunate woman." She paused to open a stubborn lid on a plastic container. She was on her own, Max mused. He'd be useless to help her.

"Since becoming a nurse, I've been to a lot of places, met some wonderful people. I told you that one of the women I cared for was a lovely, elderly lady whose goal in life was to see the world. But after she had a stroke, she needed help." A line of concentration appeared between her brows while she spooned the salad on plates. "Instead of staying home, she traveled while healing, and took me with her. Everywhere. London, Madrid, Dublin."

"Nice perk."

"Here." She offered him a bright orange plate filled with food. "Lydia opened a different world to me. I went to the symphony and operas, and in between traveling, I stayed at her estates in Acapulco and Palm Springs and learned about the finer things in life."

"Generous woman."

Curls framed her face while she dug into the basket for another colorful plate. "Yes, she was wonderful. But eccentric. She only wore purple, and had a Jack Russell terrier that went everywhere with us. I do mean everywhere. One five-star hotel in London refused to allow pets. So she had me buy a baby blanket and a baby's bonnet. With her so-called baby in her arms, I wheeled her into the hotel." A laugh rippled from her. "No one guessed."

Max had no doubt she'd been totally in step with the woman's odd ways.

"Good?" she asked as he sampled the shrimp salad.

"Everything you make is," he admitted.

She beamed and went on. "Lydia was a big influence. Because of her, I saw so much. Look," she said suddenly, and pointed toward the sky. He, too, saw the eagle gliding overhead. "That is so incredible," she said. "Since coming to live here, I've seen such wonderful sights. A black bear standing on hind legs, a bighorn sheep and now this."

Max sampled the chicken. "You weren't always a city girl," he said, assuming she had lived in Texas as Talbot had said.

"No. Mama liked to travel." Head bent, she snapped open cans of soda. "We lived in a lot of places."

"'We' meaning…?"

"There was usually a man."

"What about your father?"

She reached for her soda. "I never knew my father. I'm the daughter of Teresa Carter. Her love child. I doubt Mama ever knew who my father was. There was always a man in her life." She paused, sipped her drink. "She needed to have one."

"And that meant Joe and Ian?"

Sam released a low, husky laugh, one that sounded slightly amused. "There were more than two stepfathers. Five, actually. There was also Leo and George and Carl. She married five times. But there were other men. Some I had liked, truly missed when they'd left. One man in particular, Carl Hansen, was everything to me."

In fascination, he watched one of her silver-plated, lizard-shaped earrings sway with the movement of her head. "What made him so special?"

"I've never wondered about that. I only know that to me he was a real father."

Someone who offered normalcy? Max wondered. Security?

"We met him when we were living in Pittsburgh. He was a steelworker. A hardworking man. A sensible one. He was probably the one man Mama chose who would have given her the kind of life I wanted. Unfortunately it wasn't her kind of life. Too boring. She liked excitement. She liked change."

"So the marriage didn't last long?"

"Longer than any of the others actually. I really loved him." She smiled, but Max saw sadness in her eyes. "He used to say that I should go to school. It was important. If I wanted anything in my life, I needed to go to school. He convinced me, and I worked hard to do well."

Beneath the breeze, her hair flew forward, framing her face. Max gave in to an urge he'd had since they'd sat down. Gently he lifted strands away from her cheek. "Were you a good student?"

"A's mostly." She raised a hand and caught his to stop the stroke of his thumb on her cheek. "Has anyone told you—well, about things like that?"

Though amused by her action, Max made no comment about it and backed off for the moment. "Rachel told me that I won scholarships."

"I would have guessed that. You wouldn't like anything beating you."

That wasn't the first time she'd voiced her assessment of him. "When was he—Carl—in your life?"

"Six years. Until I was twelve. Mama met a carnival guy, and thought he'd be more interesting. Carl had a lot of pride. He wouldn't put up with her shenanigans, he'd said. So he left." She met his stare. "I wept for him then and four years later. That's when Mama learned Carl had died. He left me enough money to start college, but Mama got sick. A gallbladder attack led to an infection. When she died, I knew what I was meant to do. I still had enough money to start college, so I went to a small junior college for a year, then to a university."

"Did you plan on nursing?"

"I wanted to be a pediatrician. I love kids. But that would take too long."

Max savored the last of the chicken on his plate. "You could still do it."

"I'm content. Physical therapy is so satisfying. I liked the idea of helping people get their lives back to normal."

His mind wandered back. He'd heard nothing but affection for her mother, though the woman had never offered Sam a stable life. Recalling his lack of deep feelings about Ellis, he wondered if Sam had had the one thing in her life that his might have lacked—love.

"At first, I took all kinds of jobs," she said, coming back to his original question.

Max grabbed his soda. "What kind?"

"All kinds. I've been on my own since seventeen, working odd jobs, any kind while I went to school. I slung hash, cleaned bathrooms, stripped sheets from motel beds."

He couldn't stop himself. He had to ask. "Anything else?"

"Why would you want to know?" Puzzlement narrowed her eyes. "Is this…is this about your friend? He said that I look familiar. I don't remember him. What did he say? Did he remember where we'd met?"

"He never met you. A friend of his in Big Timber knew you—about you and your mother," he corrected.

"Really?" Her lips curved now in an enigmatic smile. "When? Where?"

"In Lubbock, Texas."

"In Lubbock." She laughed airily. "Oh, Mama was enchanted with a wildcatter named Billy Ray then." A seriousness crept back into her voice. "Who is this friend of…?"

Max supplied the name. "Talbot."

"Yes." She gazed thoughtfully at him.

Max wished he'd never begun this conversation. "Nevich. Ray Nevich."

"Oh." A spark of recognition came to her eyes. "His sister was Caroline…Caroline…" She shook her head. "I don't remember her married name. But she lived in the same trailer court. She was a well-known gossip. What did she say about us?"

"It's not important."

"Oh, but it is." A challenge edged her voice. "That's why you've been asking lots of questions, isn't it?"

"It's probably what you said. Gossip."

"Well, why don't you tell me, and I'll let you know if it's true or not."

Max wanted to forget this. The light in her eyes had faded a little.

"Go on."

There was no going back now, he knew. "Nevich told Talbot that his sister said you danced at some club."

"What club?"

Max made himself meet her stare. "The Cottontail Club."

He watched her lean away to touch a flower, a brown-eyed Susan, a bright orange flower with yellow tips. "And I suppose he told you what kind of club that was?"

"He mentioned that—"

"That the trashy Carter woman danced topless." She fixed eyes filled with displeasure on him and her chin came up, as if she dared someone to poke at it. "Is that what he said?"

"Why don't we forget—"

"No, we're not going to. I told you I worked tables to get myself through school. Your grapevine isn't very accurate. It was Mama, not me, who danced topless. I looked older than fifteen, but that's all I was when we lived in Lubbock. There was just the two of us. She always did the best she could. Maybe it wasn't what some other woman would do, but it was her way of making a life for us."

Despite the seriousness of her tone, Max nearly smiled. He admired her, admired her strength and the unconditional love she felt for her mother.

"You had a good relationship with her," he said rather than asked.

"She was fun. Mama definitely was fun. That's probably why she had so many admirers," she said, choosing a delicate phrase to explain her mother's many men. A hint of sadness slipped into her voice. "But in the end she was alone. I was there with her, of course, but all those men had passed through her life and not one of them was with her when she needed someone." She fiddled with the flower again. "All she ever wanted was love."

What about Sam? Max wondered. Why wasn't there a man in her life?

She was beautiful, an exciting-looking woman with all that red hair and those green eyes, and with skin that looked as soft as velvet. She would turn heads wherever she went. Talbot had told him that she'd been a stunner when she'd been in Texas, and she'd been only fifteen then. "This was good," he said about the food, instead of forcing more conversation about her personal life.

She gathered plates and silverware. Tension no longer held her back ramrod-straight. "Thank you."

"No dessert?"

She forgave easily, he knew, as in the next instant her short amused laugh rang on the air. "You want everything, don't you?" she teased while she maneuvered the plastic plates into the bottom of the basket. "I guess you deserve some reward for putting up with my babbling." She balled the napkins, then tossed them into the basket. "I must have bored you silly."

How wrong she was. She fascinated him. Captivated. Dazzled.

"I'm—"

Max angled toward her. With a fingertip, he outlined her top lip. "You're an interesting woman."

Sam barely took her next breath. She saw so much seriousness in his eyes. Unexpected emotion swarmed in on her. "Different," she countered quickly to keep herself from making too much of his caress.

"Interesting."

She said nothing for a moment. Was he attracted to her because she was unlike other women he knew? "You don't understand." She had to stay sensible, keep herself from getting caught up in the soft lure of his voice.

"Sure I do." Max understood too well. He'd even considered the problem himself. She really did fascinate him. How many women liked B.B. King and *Rigoletto,* cooked like a dream, traveled abroad, yet had lived in a trailer court? "We're different. You already said that."

"I'm a realist," Sam said. "I'd have pegged you as one. Wouldn't you think that, too?"

He'd like to kiss her again. He'd like more, but with no strings attached. He assumed that wouldn't work. Though complex, Sam wore her emotions for anyone to see. This wasn't the kind of woman to engage in casual affairs. He wasn't even sure it was fair to her, but resisting her proved harder every time they were together. He swore at himself even as his fingers weaved into her hair. "What's your point?"

"How can you know if I'm interesting or not to you?" He found it satisfying that she sounded a touch breathless. "You don't know yet what you like."

Sure he did—her. And he was tired of warring with himself. He'd thought he wanted nothing too involved with her because he had another life to think about, one he couldn't yet remember. But possibly he might never regain his memory. He moved his hand through her hair to the back of her neck. So how long should he wait before starting a new life? Did he even want to wait?

The answer came instantly. Not another second. Tightening his hand on her neck, he brought her face closer to his, and lowered his mouth to hers. He didn't need to know about the man he'd been. The one he was now liked her, desired her. That sounded so simple. What he was feeling wasn't. Hunger danced within him as he twisted his lips across hers. She was becoming addictive, her taste, the softness and warmth of her, her scent.

He damned the cast on his arm as desire skittered through him, made him yearn to run his hands over her. He wanted to touch her, to feel every inch of her, every curve and angle. He wanted to sink himself in her.

"Max," she murmured, and started to pull back.

He quelled a longing to keep her against him. Her chest heaving, her face flushed, she met his stare squarely. Her mouth looked swollen from his kiss, her hair mussed from when his fingers had entwined in her hair.

"Max, we need to leave."

She could pretend all she wanted, act untouched by the kiss, but he'd felt her respond. There was little he knew for certain, but he had no trouble with feelings. She wanted him, too. He'd felt that.

He watched her scramble to a stand. Thunder rumbled in the distance. Overhead, dark clouds gathered, growing more threatening. "It's going to rain," she said as an excuse for rushing away and grabbed the handles of the basket.

Max banked his craving, resisted pulling her back down and against him. Some other time, he told himself. Standing near, she braced her feet to help him. He took the hand she offered. Some other time. Soon.

It poured before they reached the house and was still raining the next morning.

After the day they'd spent together, she thought it best to put some space between Max and herself. Definitely what she'd felt for him had become more confusing. No clear-cut definition such as employer and employee or patient and nurse worked anymore. And she needed time alone, time to think about what had been happening. Except for sharing a quick breakfast with him, she kept her distance. While he closeted himself in the den, she spent the morning trying to read a book.

Her mind kept wandering to yesterday. She'd answered his kiss, she admitted. She'd melted beneath it, yearned for more. His mouth could have ravaged hers, and she would still have felt dissatisfied, longing for more. She simply couldn't get enough of him.

So now what? What should she do? She didn't want to give up the job. Professional pride was at stake. She'd never quit any job before. She was not a quitter, never had been or would be. For too many years she'd watched her mother quit relationships on a whim and become a loser in love.

In retrospect, Sam knew that was her mother's fault. She'd never considered tomorrow, what she'd feel for the man when she wasn't in his arms. Only today had mattered to her. Sam wouldn't make the same mistakes.

But not just Max's kiss bothered her. Her reaction to him disturbed her. Why had she said so much to him earlier? Rarely did she talk about her mother, her youth. It wasn't that she was ashamed of her background, but relaying Mama's plentiful love life never made a good impression on people.

As a child, she'd listened to kids' taunts. "Trailer trash," several of her schoolmates had chanted. "Your mama's a whore," she'd heard more than once. To Sam, it hadn't mattered what they'd said. Sure the words had hurt, but no one could make her love her mother less.

As an adult, Sam had understood better that her mother, who'd known too many foster homes as a child, had been searching for something she'd never had—love. And while Sam lacked a lot of other things during her youth, she'd always had love. Always.

But that part of her life had been private before this. What about Max had made her share so much? Perhaps knowing how much he wanted to learn about himself, how vulnerable he was, had opened her up.

Seven

Sam had hopes of getting positive feedback from one of Max's employees. After lunch she meandered into the kitchen and smiled with pleasure at the sight of Foster, Max's chauffeur. She'd been looking forward to getting acquainted with him. Louise, too shy and timid to complain, managed her employment for Max by avoiding him. Martin claimed Mr. Montgomery usually left him to make decisions about the landscaping, and when Gibson was around, he ran the household.

"Mr. Montgomery is fair," Foster told her when she took a chair opposite him at the table. He was an amiable man in his sixties with salt-and-pepper-colored hair. "He's paying, so he has a right to expect certain things. I like him. And Gibson would do anything for him."

"But his last cook—"

"Della was lazy," Foster said without a second's hesitation. "Give him a day's worth of work, and you'll have no problem."

Sam simply nodded. Max's reputation for being an ogre seemed undeserved. Obviously most of his employees did like working for him.

After Foster left, she busied herself with preparing the evening's dinner, a Mexican smorgasbord of tamales and enchiladas and tacos.

She was nearly finished with cleaning up when she heard the doorbell. Curious, she stepped into the hallway that led toward the foyer, then peeked around a corner. Jack Henderson, Rachel's husband, was talking to Max. The tall, ruggedly handsome private investigator suited Max's sister so perfectly.

Assuming he and Max would visit, Sam decided to take a walk. She slid on her rain slicker, then opened the refrigerator and removed a casserole dish filled with some of the homemade tamales.

Unmindful of the rain, she strolled toward Max's closest neighbors, the Crowleys, Joe and Barbara. After giving Barbara the casserole with the tamales, she joined the woman and her husband in the kitchen. While she ate a slice of Barbara's applesauce cake, she listened to their stories about their three grown children, ten grandchildren and one great-grandchild.

"We raised our children here, but they left for big cities," Joe said. "That's okay. They didn't get uppity like some people I know."

"Joe, shh," Barbara scolded.

"What? She must know what he's like. She works for him. He's too good to even say hello, to wave or anything."

Sam said nothing out of loyalty to Max, but she couldn't defend him, either. "I'd like to come again," she said when they were walking to the door later.

"Anytime," Barbara answered.

For a moment Sam bent and pet their dog, a fluffy, soft collie mix. It nuzzled her hand with its cold nose.

"Sheba just had puppies. When you come back, you'll have to see them," Barbara said with the warmth of an old friend.

Sam raised the hood on her rain slicker. "I'd like that." They were nice people, she thought while heading back to Max's house. So why had Max kept his distance? Or had he done that with everyone out of habit?

She stayed at the Crowleys' longer than she planned, and with the rain, darkness came earlier. She noticed Jack's car still parked in the driveway. She offered both men dinner. Jack refused; Max said he'd heat his later.

Sam warmed up food for herself, ate, then after getting a cup of coffee, she took a book she'd been reading earlier and settled in the living room.

At midnight she awakened to a dark house and to find a blanket covering her. Good job, Sam, she berated herself. She was supposed to take care of him, not vice versa. Muttering, she went to Max's room and quietly opened the door.

Still dressed, he'd fallen asleep on top of the covers. Sam listened to his soft snoring. In the shadowed light, he looked so restful, so trusting, lying on his back, one arm under his head. She soaked up the sight of his features, peaceful with sleep, his dark hair slightly tousled.

She could fall in love with him, she realized.

Love? *Oh, Sam, what are you doing?* She knew love's pitfalls. So many men had passed through her mother's and her life. At its best, even when two people were perfectly suited to each other, love was tough to hold on to. So why was she even thinking about it with Max?

The idea of her being in love with him was ludicrous, she tried to tell herself the next morning as she drove Max to doctors' appointments. She might have convinced herself if she didn't enjoy being with him, talking to him. But they'd spent a fun morning together, filled with laughter as he'd shared Jack's stories about little Alyssa. If she felt such pleasure even when not in his arms, how could she reassure herself that what she felt was simply lust?

"You're quiet."

She felt him studying her and glanced over, saw his smile. "I'd think you'd be pleased," she said on a laugh. "You always say I talk too much."

"I'm getting used to it." A softness had entered his gaze. He hadn't moved, but she felt as if he'd narrowed the space between them.

Every minute she was with him, she simply wanted to go with her feelings. Heartbreak road ahead, Sam mused.

"Sam, don't be so quiet. It makes me nervous."

He made her laugh. He did that often. "You have to decide which way you want it," she teased.

"Blabber."

"Okay." She worked at relaxing herself. "You have back-to-back appointments today, Mr. Montgomery. The second one is with—"

"The local shrink from Whitehorn Memorial, I know."

Clearly he disliked the idea, but his doctor had thought the visits might be best until Max's memory returned.

"I could do without all the doctors."

"Everyone feels that way, Max, unless they really need them."

"The accident was dumb. My fault."

Sam allowed another look away from the traffic. "A memory?"

"People have told me I was driving on the road that bisects the woods. At first, they thought I took a curve too fast. I guess I have a heavy foot." Amusement entered his voice. "Not as heavy as yours." He turned a meaningful look on the speedometer. "But the accident report verified that I wasn't speeding."

"Do you remember that?"

"My memory comes in snatches. Sometimes someone will say something, and I'll remember a moment, a face."

How hard this was for him, Sam thought not for the

first time. As sunshine streaked out from behind one of the dark, drifting clouds, she lowered her visor. "Like what?"

"Like Foster," he said about the chauffeur. "He told me that my butler had a terrible poker face. I remembered Gibson then. If he got a good hand, he'd grin."

"You remember playing poker with them?" She felt thrilled for him. "That's terrific. That's great progress. You've had more than a flash of a memory. Where did you play the game? Do you remember that?"

"In the kitchen. Gibson drank tonic water, and Foster and I had imported Irish brew."

Sam heard pleasure in his voice. It occurred to her how few encouraging moments like this he'd had. "Did you play for money?"

"Foster and Gibson played for days off. If they won, they got days off with pay, and if they lost, they'd forfeit free hours."

"You're tough, Montgomery," she said on a laugh. "Remind me not to play poker with you." Sam slowed the car as she turned onto the town's main street. "So about the accident. If you weren't speeding, what caused the accident?"

"A fawn. It froze on the road."

"That you remember?"

"That I remember," he confirmed.

"Do you know if you hit it?"

"I didn't. And according to Rachel, I wouldn't. She told me that I wanted to be a veterinarian when I was a kid."

Sam considered what he'd said. Life certainly had taken him down an opposite road from that of a doctor who cared and wanted to heal. "Why didn't you become a vet?"

"I told you. I was a kid when I wanted to be one."

Sam wondered if he had regrets. Did a person ever outgrow some childhood dreams? "Did you have lots of animals?"

"I asked my family that." He looked away from the scenery and toward her now. "I never even had a dog."

His words saddened her. She'd had a stray mutt—a Heinz 57—and a goldfish.

"By the time I was thirteen," he continued, "according to Ellis, I wanted to follow in his footsteps and be a banker."

Sam couldn't stop a thought. Was that because he wanted to or because it was expected of him? "I wonder if you planned to go into politics like him."

"I have no idea."

She noted he'd returned to staring hard at the passing stores, intent on remembering. She left him to his thoughts while she parked the car.

As other memories, this one was a breakthrough. Sam eased out of the car, then strolled around it to join Max on the sidewalk. "I'll walk with you to the doctor's office."

"Samantha—"

The exasperation in his voice halted her. "You don't want me to go with you?" Looking past him, she saw Janie in the Hip Hop, watching them through the floor-to-ceiling front window.

Max traced her stare, then motioned toward the Hip Hop. "Go have coffee and I'll meet you when I'm done."

Sam acquiesced. "Okay, this time." She really didn't have to go with him. Only when the cast came off should she go along for the doctor's orders.

Before stepping around her, he smiled and brushed his knuckles affectionately over her cheek. It was such a simple touch, not sexual, not provocative. But the caring touch stroked more than her skin, it caressed her heart. And everything changed in that second. She couldn't deny what was true. It felt right to be with him, as if during every other second in her life she'd been waiting for this kind of special closeness with someone. She watched while Max strode away, then turned toward the café door. As she opened it, she hoped she wasn't wearing a silly grin.

"I don't believe it," one of the waitresses quipped. She propped a hand on her hip and stared out the window at Max, who was crossing the street. Slowly she shook her head and slanted a look at a customer. "Did you see that?" she asked with amazement in her voice. "Max Montgomery smiled."

The customer played along. "I thought I'd imagined that."

Sam laughed at them, and nodded agreeably to Janie when she held up the coffeepot.

"Guess you're not having as much trouble with him as others have," another voice piped in. Lily Mae Wheeler, Whitehorn's one-woman gossip line, always offered her opinion.

"Watch out, Samantha," Janie warned. "Lily May will pump you until you reveal every secret you know."

"Oh, go on," Lily murmured good-naturedly, waving her bejeweled hands in the air. A flamboyant-looking woman in her sixties, she'd recently changed the color of her hair. This month it rivaled the orange in the carrots on her plate.

"Hi, Samantha."

Samantha jerked around, along with Lily Mae.

"It's been so long since I've seen you." Lori Parker Bains was one of the prettiest women Sam knew, with her blond hair and her toothpaste-ad smile, but Sam had never known the woman well. Lori was actually best friends with Maris Wyler Rivers, owner of a nearby ranch. Sam had become acquainted with Lori, a midwife nurse, during the blizzard rescue several winters ago. Any medical staff available had answered the call for help. While Lori had offered assurances to a woman who'd started labor that she would reach the hospital in time, Samantha had assisted a doctor in stabilizing a young man's broken leg.

Sam hadn't seen Lori since a celebration of sorts over coffee and donuts offered by grateful townspeople to the medical volunteers after everyone was safe.

"It's wonderful to see you again. And under better circumstances." Sam gestured toward the booth. "Why don't you sit down?"

"For a little while." Lori slid into the booth with Sam. "Did that young boy do all right?"

"He healed fine." Sam looked up and nodded a

thank-you to Janie as she set a cup of coffee in front of her. "What about the baby?" she asked.

"He was born that night." Lori's face glowed suddenly. "They named him Jordan Parker Weston. After me. I was thrilled."

Samantha imagined Lori received a lot of satisfaction in her work. "Are you and Travis still at the ranch?" she asked about Lori's handsome husband.

"Ranching is his life."

Sam recalled Lori had three daughters. "And your girls. They must be getting so big."

"Are they ever. The twins are growing so fast that I can hardly believe it. I'd like to spend more time with them." Lori pulled a face. "But we don't have hoards of money like some people."

Sam raised her eyes from the dark brew in her coffee cup. What was that about?

"I heard you're working for the Montgomerys now."

First Lori had mentioned money, then the name Montgomery. Sam understood now. This conversation was about who she was working for. "It's a temporary position. Max Montgomery had a car accident and suffered a broken arm and amnesia."

"Amnesia? That's...that's awful, isn't it?"

"Yes, I don't think it's easy for him."

"You know the reason I mentioned the Montgomerys is because I had something to do with his sister."

Sam paid attention. Where was she going with this conversation. "Rachel?"

"Oh, no." Lori hunched forward toward Sam and spoke conspiratorially. "The other one. Christina."

"What do you mean, you had something to do with her?"

"That's what the police wanted to know," she said in a tone that indicated she was inflated with self-importance because of some information she had. "That's where I just came from—the police station. The police wanted to talk to me about Christina Montgomery."

Impatience rushed Sam suddenly. She wished Lori would tell her whatever it was that made her think she was an authority about Christina Montgomery.

"She was pregnant, you know. I examined her. I knew she was."

Since Rachel had the baby, Sam found nothing news-breaking about Lori's words. Everyone knew by now that Christina had been pregnant. When a baby had been left with Rachel, gossip had been rampant that the baby must be Christina Montgomery's. The father's identity remained a secret. But Sam had learned like everyone else that Rachel had had the baby tested and the DNA proved it was Christina's.

In town, speculation had risen. Was the pregnancy—that precious child—the reason Christina was murdered? Had some man wanted his identity kept secret and killed her to prevent her from naming him?

"Why did the police call you in?" Sam asked. "Did Christina tell you the name of the baby's father?"

"They didn't call me. I volunteered."

For Max's sake, Sam thought it best to learn all that

she could. If some new development existed in solving his sister's murder, Sam believed he needed to hear about it from someone mindful of his condition, someone who cared. "Did she tell you the name of the baby's father?"

"Well, no, she didn't, not exactly."

Sam's patience waned. Perhaps Lori knew nothing and was simply on a self-importance kick. Annoyance and exasperation welling up within her, Sam looked away, ready to end the conversation and to make an escape.

"I think—" Lori leaned in and whispered, "I think he's a Native American."

Sam wondered if Lori had some facts or was just voicing her opinion.

"Why?" a male voice suddenly asked.

Like Sam, Lori jerked toward the sound.

Max stood beside the booth and eyed Lori with wariness.

"You're done already?" Sam questioned.

"The appointment was postponed for half an hour," he answered, but hadn't looked away from Lori. "Why did you say that?"

Concern for him rushed through Sam. When had he come in? How much had he overheard?

"What did Christina say?" he prodded.

"Oh, Mr. Montgomery, I didn't know you were here."

Max cut her off from saying more. "What did she say?" he asked again.

He could intimidate with a look, Sam acknowledged, and wondered if she was catching a glimpse of the man who'd earned a reputation as unyielding.

From an adjoining table, he swung around a chair, then straddled it. "Tell me," he insisted.

In a small show of nerves, Lori curled her purse strap around several fingers. "When I was done with the examination and confirmed that Christina was pregnant, she laughed." Lori's brows bunched. "No, that's not right. It wasn't really a laugh. 'Daddy won't be happy,' she'd said."

Sam imagined that was true. With his campaign ahead of him, Ellis would have viewed his youngest daughter's pregnancy, especially without benefit of marriage, as untimely.

"I said that being a grandpa might change his mind. You know, I was trying to make her feel better. Once he sees the baby, he'll be happy, I'd said." Lori turned from Max to Samantha then. "I've seen that happen before. Everyone is upset, but sometimes when they see the baby, no one cares if the girl was married or not. A baby makes everyone feel good."

"Did she feel better then?" Sam asked, wondering about Christina's state of mind.

Distress deepened the lines bracketing Lori's mouth.

"I don't think so." She glanced Max's way. "I'm sorry. But she acted as if I'd given her really bad news, though she laughed. Not a funny laugh. It was one of those high-pitched ones that sound more sad than happy. And she said more to herself than me,

'Daddy will never welcome this grandchild with open arms.'"

Across the table, Max's eyes met Samantha's before he asked Lori, "Why? Did she explain what she meant?"

"Ellis—" Lori paused and focused on Max. "She used the name Ellis, not daddy. 'Ellis Montgomery never took kindly to Cheyennes,' she said." Lori nodded her head as if confirming her words. "That's what she said. That's what I told the police. And I heard they'd questioned Gavin Nighthawk."

Expressionless, his head bent, Max kept his gaze fixed on some youth's initials etched in the table.

"Guess, I'll go." Lori stood and waited a second.

As if lost in deep thought, Max didn't look up.

"'Bye," Sam said to urge Lori to leave.

"I believe her," Max said softly when they were alone.

Sam swayed closer to keep their conversation private. "What do you believe?"

"About Ellis. More than once, when he'd talked about his campaign, he'd made comments that sounded prejudiced."

"If that's true, then do you think what else she said is true?"

"Seems likely." Max frowned. "Who is Gavin Nighthawk? Do you know?"

"He's a resident at the hospital." Sam couldn't give him more information. "I don't know him personally. I only know what I've heard about him."

"And that's what?"

"I know he left the Laughing Horse Reservation for college and medical school. He's conscientious, determined to make a name for himself as a surgeon."

"Was Christina involved with him?"

"I don't know who she was seeing." She hated gossiping about Christina. It seemed wrong. Christina could hardly defend herself, but Sam answered what was public knowledge. "She had a reputation as a flirt, Max."

With her words, Sam became aware of whispering at the next table. She made a half turn and saw the source. Lily Mae's mouth flapped away to Janie. She'd heard too much. Soon everyone in town would hear the latest about Christina. "Lily Mae will spread Lori's words all over town," Sam warned Max.

"I don't care. What difference does it make?"

"I think your father will be upset by the gossip."

Max merely shrugged. Appearing indifferent, he said no more and left for his doctors' appointments.

Unlike Max, his father and sister would be affected by this latest news, Sam believed.

Later that afternoon, as she was driving through the gates outside Max's home, she considered his quieter mood. The moment they'd gotten into the car, he'd switched on the CD player. For most of the ride, he seemed content to pass time listening to saxophone music. Sam didn't intrude until they neared the house. "Did the doctor say you're doing well?"

"Uh, huh." He answered in a distracted manner.

Sam saw why as she spotted a man and woman standing on the driveway. "Those are your neighbors. The Crowleys."

"Neighbors?"

"They're really nice, Max." Since grumpiness came easily to him, she hoped he acted civil. Perhaps if he developed a friendship with them, it would remain after his amnesia was gone. She stopped near the front door. Instead of waiting for Max, she bounded from the car to greet Joe and Barbara. With some reluctance, Max joined them.

Barbara delivered a weak smile in his direction. "I brought you something," she said to Sam. "Joe—" she motioned with her thumb at her husband "—ate every single tamale you brought over, Samantha." Affectionately she touched Sam's arm. "So I brought you my lasagna. Everyone says it's really good. I hope you like it."

Sam accepted the dish from her. "How sweet of you."

Barbara eyed Max then. "We heard you hit your head. We hope you feel better soon, Mr. Montgomery."

"Thanks."

"You're welcome," Barbara responded with an uncertain smile.

Joe hooked his hand under his wife's elbow. "Let's go now." He propelled Barbara away from them. "Hope it knocked some sense into him."

"Apparently I'm not his favorite person," Max said when the Crowleys were out of hearing range.

Sam didn't buy his indifferent act. She'd seen his frown. He could be stoic and blasé with others, but she'd noticed the discomfort, even pain and embarrassment in his eyes whenever someone revealed a past incident and a less than sterling image of him. Not wanting him to be alone to brood, Sam followed him into the den. "Max, you're upset, aren't you?"

"About me," he answered simply.

If only she could make this easier for him. "Max, don't be hard on yourself." Tenderly she caressed his cheek. "It's who you are now that's important."

She saw what looked like sorrow in his eyes. "And who's that?" he asked.

Sam's heart ached for him. Always he faced the emptiness of his own mind. "I like him. A lot," she said softly. No, she felt more. Consequences suddenly didn't matter. She was, she realized, her mother's daughter, after all.

A hint of a smile crept into his eyes. In a loverlike way, he placed a hand at the curve of her waist. "Was that said as nurse to patient?"

Sam's heart thudded harder. No amount of resistance worked. She was falling in love with him, rough edges and all. Tilting her face up to him, she welcomed his embrace. "Woman to man," she said quietly. With a gentleness that was so light she barely felt it, his hand roamed over the curve of her breast.

"I love the perfume you wear." He kissed the throbbing pulse at her throat. "You put it right here. Where else?"

Sam couldn't talk. In what seemed to take effort, she looked down and saw her partially opened blouse. With one hand he'd deftly opened the top two buttons. "Max," she said, breathless.

He kissed her cheek, the bridge of her nose. Slowly he rained kisses over her face. "Do you want me to stop?"

Of course, she didn't.

She clung to his shoulders and responded with a tease. "Sometimes you talk too much," she murmured.

Eight

His laugh answered her. His hand at her face, he kissed her with a feather-light seduction. It was a deliberate move, she guessed. An enticement. And it worked. She was dying inside for a fuller taste, for another deep, stirring kiss, for the heat and wildness she'd felt in his last kiss.

Desire hummed through her as his hand skimmed beneath her blouse, cupping her breast again. She framed his face with her hands. She needed him. He was the one who'd make her feel complete. He was the one.

When his mouth captured hers, pleasure instantly exploded within her. As if to stamp his mark on her, his lips pressed harder on hers. Eyes closed, she absorbed his taste, drifted beneath the magic of the kiss. This seemed inevitable to her. To him, too? she wondered. Had they been marking time until this moment?

Sam wedged her hands between them, fumbled with the buttons of his shirt. As it parted, she splayed her fingers over the sleek smoothness, glided them up from the hard plane of his stomach to his chest.

What sounded like a laugh edged his voice. "We'll never make it to the bedroom."

"We could stay here," she said unevenly as she dragged the shirt off him. She'd seen him naked before, but this moment was different. When the shirt fell to the floor, she gripped his bare shoulders, let her fingers dance across the hard contours, the tautness of his flesh.

Beneath her hand on his chest, she felt the quickened beat of his heart. She had no thought but of the moment. She answered the play of his lips, the moist touch of his tongue. Her mind emptied to everything else. Not wanting to think of anything but his taste, she invited his seduction, the madness it could sweep her toward.

The coolness in the den rippled across her bare back when he eased her blouse off one shoulder, then the other. She felt such gentleness in his touch, in the kiss on her collarbone.

Her heart pounding, she yanked at the buttons on his jeans. With a long, low moan, she pushed at the denim and felt him quiver in response to the brush of her knuckles on his belly. Even before they stood naked, before he pulled her down to the rug with him, she was lost in him. Warm pleasure kindled within her. She felt the beat of his heart against her, heard the soft, intimate tone of his voice enticing her.

Eyes shut now, she fed on his urgency, on the sensations slithering along her flesh. She shifted to her side to give him room to explore. He scooted down, his lips trailing the length of her ribs to the curve of her hip.

She sprang alive beneath his kiss at her navel and sucked in air as his breath, hot and quick, fanned the inside of her thigh. Nothing existed except her body, the warmth of his mouth. With each exquisite stroke of his tongue, pleasure skittered through her, stole the breath from her, hurled her into a world of ecstasy. There was only him. She called his name while the sensation, the swift head-to-toe shudder, swept through her. Had she ever longed this much? she wondered. She wanted to rest, to catch her breath, but she didn't want to let go of him. On a moan, she clung to him as if he were her lifeline.

Breathless, hot, her skin damp, she slowly opened her eyes. He was face-to-face with her again. For one heart-stopping second, his gaze met hers. Trust. Need. Desire. She saw all of that in his eyes.

"In my wallet," he said in a husky tone, and started to pull away from her. He swore, hindered from movement by his cast.

Just as impatient, Sam took over. She reached for his jeans and in the wallet, she found the foil package.

"Here, give it to me."

Anything, she thought. But not yet. She slowed the moment, nudged him to his back. Braced over him, Sam kissed his chest, let her tongue circle a nipple, roam the rock-hard surface of his belly, seek the heat and hardness of him.

She wanted to please him. She wanted to flirt with his control. She traced her fingertips along the curves of his arms, along his ribs. She kissed, she tasted. She loved.

His fingers grabbed a handful of her hair. There was no pull. He simply held on as if he needed to grip something to keep from falling. She taunted him, raining kisses over his body, memorizing every inch of it until she felt his muscles quiver. With his low moan, she rose above him.

Her eyes never left his as she straddled his thighs. With trembling hands, she rolled the protection over him, then inched forward. Head back, she slowly took the length of him into her. There was him, only him, the warmth and fullness of him, the strong feel of his hand gripping her hip now. Waves of sensation flooding her, she moved with and against him. A fire for him burned within her.

She heard another low moan—this time her own. Then his arm pressed against her back, tightened her to him as if he'd never let her go. It didn't matter if that was true or not. For a little while, she wanted to believe it.

Her body damp and flushed, she listened to his breathing, as harsh and quick as her own, and lay still on top of him while her heartbeat slowed to a normal beat.

Beneath the darkness in the den, she could see his face, his features less fierce now, almost serene. "I'll move," she said as she felt him shift slightly beneath her.

"Stay."

Content, she rested her cheek against his chest and shut her eyes. She had one thought then.

One night was not enough.

Slowly Sam opened her eyes. The faint light of dawn flowed into the den, but she wasn't ready to get up. Aware of the warm body beside her, she closed her eyes and curled in the crook of Max's arm, absorbing his scent with every breath she took. She had no regrets, never expected to have any. She might seem spontaneous, but she tended to mull over notions almost endlessly before taking action. To be with him had been no spur-of-the-moment decision. She'd fantasized about it overlong.

Her fantasies had paled in comparison. She'd always thought she had an amazingly fertile imagination. But she'd never have conjured up such a wonderful night with him.

It had been perfect, and she hoped he wouldn't want to talk about it, wouldn't spoil the memory for her. She wanted this day with him. No explanations. No questions.

Shifting, she propped her chin on her hand and took her fill of his sleek, muscular body while he slept. Was such thinking head-in-the-sand mentality? Probably. But what her head knew hardly mattered. He'd touched her heart.

Feather-light, she kissed his shoulder. Though tempted to stay beside him, to curl into him, she eased from the sofa bed they'd opened during the night. On her way to the door, she snatched up clothes that had been discarded in haste last night, and carried the bundle up the stairs to her room, aware she'd have only a few moments before he would be up. Usually he didn't laze around. He showered, dressed, drank two cups of coffee and a glass of juice and usually devoured the newspaper from front to back in the first hour.

After dressing, Sam returned to the den to set jeans and a shirt for him on a chair. If he awakened before she came back and he wanted to dress, he could manage. As she had done the other night, she watched him sleeping. With his breathing slow and steady, he looked at peace, so approachable. Bending forward, she brushed her lips across his, then covered him with a blanket before turning her thoughts to breakfast.

She wandered into the kitchen and, after starting the coffee, she removed several eggs from the refrigerator.

He was brave, far braver than others realized, she reflected. Unlike some patients, he'd held back complaints, never gave in to self-pity. He must be scared once in a while. Late at night while in the bed and the darkness, with only his own thoughts for company, fear must come close to overwhelming him. But he'd never let anyone see that. So in a way, the man he'd been—the private and sometimes unyielding and sometimes demanding man—still existed. And that man gave him the strength to get through the difficult times.

She loved that man, too. He wasn't perfect. He brooded. He was sometimes cranky. He was often too quiet. But Max—the old and the new—was her "Mr. Right."

Behind her, the coffeemaker hissed loudly with the final drops as a bluesy rendition of "It Had To Be You" drifted from the radio.

Bright sunlight streaked between the venetian blinds in the den when Max opened his eyes. Though half asleep, he'd known when Sam had left him. The room had been cast in the light of gray dawn. After she'd covered him with a blanket, her lips had brushed his. The instant she'd left, he'd missed her.

Missed her? He hadn't expected to find more than sex with her, but whatever he was feeling went beyond the physical storm she brewed within him with a simple touch. He'd wanted to pleasure her, give her a gentleness he'd only just discovered he possessed.

He didn't think she would expect anything this morning. She hadn't looked for promises from him last night. But where did they go from here? What could he offer her?

Spotting his clothes, he crossed the room and began dressing. For the first time since he'd awakened in that hospital room not knowing his name, he didn't feel alone. Someone special was in his life.

With no clear-cut answer, he ambled toward the kitchen, lured there by the deep, rich smell of coffee. Music—the sound of Pete Fountain and his clarinet playing a Dixieland classic—came from the kitchen.

Max stopped at the doorway, braced his shoulder against the doorjamb and enjoyed the sight of her moving around the sunny, bright room, the telephone receiver glued to her ear.

Her back to him, she kept her attention on the French toast browning in the frying pan. "I'll tell Max," she said to the caller.

He waited until she set down the phone. She stood now in the softness of morning sunlight, and without doing anything, she enticed him. He moved behind her, crowding her. "Tell me what?"

On a laugh, she turned, her eyes filled with a warm glow. He thought she looked happy, content. He sure as hell was. "That was Rachel," she told him. "She called to tell us that she hired a cook."

Because he needed contact of some kind, he kissed the side of her neck. "When will she start?" He could have told her that he was satisfied with the meals she'd made, but he supposed asking Sam to handle the duty wasn't fair.

"Tomorrow. Rachel told her to arrive at six in the morning. That way she can make breakfast."

"Is this someone I know?" He stepped back to pour himself coffee. He hoped it was a stranger, someone who didn't have a history with him. He was tired of feeling guilty because he couldn't remember people.

"She used to work for a state senator's family, but her daughter lives in town, so she wanted to find a job near her. Rachel assured the woman that she wouldn't have to live-in unless it was agreeable to her. She doesn't, does she?"

"No. That's fine." Actually to give Samantha and him more privacy, he would prefer that she didn't. A laugh nearly slipped out. Amazing. He'd linked them together as if they were a couple. Did he have a right to want that? Could he be with her later—after he regained his memory?

"Your sister would like to come over later."

"Her and Jack?" He'd first met his brother-in-law while he'd been in the hospital and had instantly liked him. Though Max couldn't recall their friendship, he planned to encourage one.

"Uh-uh. Jack is with his sister, Gina. They work together, as private investigators."

Max didn't remember her. What had the doctor told him? His memory could return any minute. Or not, he mused.

"Anyway, she and Alyssa will be coming over."

Max set his cup on the table as Sam came near with a pitcher of warm syrup. He hadn't seen Christina's baby yet.

At the stove again, Sam slid the French toast onto plates. "Rachel said to let her know if you don't want visitors today."

Thoughtfully he stared at her. "I wonder if I always made her call before she came over."

"Probably."

Max didn't miss her teasing grin. "Why do you think so?"

"'The handsomest stuffed shirt I ever saw'—that's what Lily Mae said about you."

"Should I consider that a compliment or be insulted?"

"Considering that it came from Lily Mae, I'd take it as a compliment. The newspaper is there," she said, indicating a nearby chair.

He couldn't care less. Out the window he saw Louise and Martin arriving. Above the garage, the apartment windows of the chauffeur's quarters were open. Foster would be coming outside soon. Rachel would be arriving with the little one, and all he could think about was being alone with Sam. He stepped up behind her again, and placed a hand on her belly, then pulled her back against him.

Laughter flooded her voice. "If you keep fooling around, we'll never eat."

"Fooling around?" How slim she felt beneath his hands. How quickly, with a simple touch on her, she made him feel desperate. He caressed her hair, pushing strands back so he could nibble her ear. "I thought I showed more finesse," he whispered, and reached around her to switch off the burner. "Breakfast will reheat in the microwave, won't it?"

On another laugh, she turned in his embrace. "Definitely."

* * *

By the time they left the bedroom, the house was no longer quiet. Louise was dusting in the formal dining room, Foster was washing the limo, and Martin was trimming a hedge.

Using the kitchen phone, Max called his sister, made arrangements for her to come at ten, then joined Sam at the kitchen table.

Sam felt as if she belonged here, but it occurred to her that he didn't. Probably before his amnesia, he'd never sat at the kitchen table, had never eaten in this room.

Rachel confirmed that thought when she came to visit. "I can't believe you're still having breakfast." She gave the clock on the wall a quick check. "It's kind of late for you, isn't it?" She sent a questioning look from Max to Sam and back to him. "Never mind. If you want to sleep late, that's your business. But I was surprised to find you in here."

"It was time for a change."

"Time for a lot of things." A seriousness clouded Rachel's eyes for a second. "I thought you should know. I heard that the police are doing a DNA test on Gavin Nighthawk."

"The doctor?"

"Yes."

"This could be a wild-goose chase."

Rachel nodded agreeably. "Yes, it could."

"We'll know soon enough." Max finished the last of the French toast on his plate. "Where's the little one?"

"Alyssa was sleeping so I left her in her infant seat in the dining room by Louise. I'll get her."

"No. We'll go to her."

As Max rose to his feet and shoved back his chair, Sam went to the sink. She plunged her hands into the soapy dishwater. "I'll finish cleaning up and do the dishes first."

Across the room, her eyes met his. Go, she silently seemed to say. Max understood. He needed time alone with Rachel. Though he didn't know what their relationship had been before his amnesia, he hoped for a closeness with her now. "We didn't see each other often, did we?" he asked when he fell in step with Rachel in the foyer.

"Hardly ever."

Max relied on her honesty. "My fault?"

"We both led our own lives for a while, Max." She touched his arm. "I wasn't living here. I was living in Chicago. I didn't come back until Christina disappeared. It was no one's fault we grew so far apart."

Bending over the baby in the carrier, Rachel pulled down the white-and-pink blanket covering her. "This is Alyssa." A sound of deep devotion came into her voice.

Small and wrinkled, with delicate features, her eyes squeezed tight, Alyssa bowed her little mouth. Max wished her eyes were open.

Tenderly Rachel stroked the soft dark hair on Alyssa's head. "I hope the next time we come she's awake."

Wanting contact, Max curled a gentle hand over Rachel's shoulder. "I'd like to spend time with her."

"Whenever you want." She caught his hand. "Come on. I brought photo albums with me." She led him toward the sofa. "I thought they might help you remember something."

Sam busied herself in the kitchen. When she thought enough time had passed, she carried a tray with coffee to them. "Can I join the party now?" she asked from the doorway. "I brought some plum cake."

In the manner of a good friend, Rachel offered a huge smile. "Oh, I wish I could stay, but I have an appointment at the salon in town."

While Max walked his sister to her car, Sam stood outside the front door. Waving to Rachel, she waited for Max to come back to her.

His eyes danced with some private amusement. "She asked if I was sleeping with you."

Sam lifted a brow. "What did you say?"

He laced his fingers with hers. "I told her I don't want to know about her sex life, so why would she want to know about mine?"

Sam tsked. "That's as good as an admittance."

"Probably."

Sam inched against him. "Was she upset with you?"

"She laughed." Lightly he kissed the side of her neck. "Didn't you offer some of that plum cake?"

"Ah, that's why you're smooching me."

His lips hovered above hers now. "'Smooching you'?"

"You have a thing for sweets, don't you?"

"Always," Max whispered before closing his mouth over hers.

His lips didn't tease. There was a new heat, a familiar thoroughness to his kiss now. All that Sam had felt last night with him seemed only a breath away. He could take her, here, in the middle of the front doorway, in daylight with anyone watching—if she hadn't heard the noise. The purr of a car engine made its way through the haze slipping over her. Reluctantly she pulled back to see a white compact car on the driveway. "You have company," she said. The driver, a thin man in his late twenties, was a stranger to Samantha. "I don't know who that is."

Though more interested in running a light trail of kisses along her jaw, Max briefly looked up. "An employee from the bank bringing me work," he muttered against her cheek.

"You're finding yourself," she teased. "Everyone said you're a workaholic."

"I'm not."

Sam nearly closed her eyes when his tongue stroked her earlobe. "Of course you are."

"I'll prove it. We'll do whatever you want after he leaves." Gently he nibbled at the sensitive lobe. "I won't even open the folders."

"Of course you won't," she said dubiously, pulling away while she still could.

Max followed her stride from him until she disappeared into the dining room. A sense of something lost skittered through him. Damn. She'd only stepped away and he was yearning for her. He had it bad for a wild redhead. He'd like to excuse it to fascination with her quirky sense of humor. Or the allure of those incredible green eyes. He could say he was captivated by the whole package. Who knew? All he knew for sure was that she'd become important to him.

"Mrs. Redden asked that I drop these off," the young man from the car said with his approach, intruding on Max's thoughts. "I'm one of the loan officers, Mr. Montgomery. Greg Kanish." Studious-looking, with a slightly receding hairline, he stared at Max through thick-lensed, dark-rimmed glasses.

Max noted the manila folders he'd taken from the briefcase. "Thank you for bringing these files."

"You're welcome, sir. If that's all, I'll…I'll leave then."

Max accepted the folders and riffled through them for one in particular. "Wait a minute. Where's the Hutchinson file?"

"The—" Kanish's Adam's apple bobbed. "I thought— It's not there?" He crossed back to Max in a few strides. "I was certain I'd brought that one with me. I—I'll go back to the bank, sir. I'll be back with it in a few minutes. Would that be all right?"

"Relax." Max studied figures on one sheet. "Greg, it's no real problem. Edna—Mrs. Redden, is coming tomorrow. Remind her to bring it with her."

"Thank you, Mr. Montgomery."

Max ended his perusal of statistics. An unpleasant

feeling coursed through him. Kanish scurried away, but Max gathered Greg would have bowed if he thought it would help. What the hell was the problem? Needing answers, Max picked up the phone on the foyer table and punched out Edna's number at the bank. A call to her should clear up his questions. "He seemed downright fearful that he'd lose his job because he forgot a bring the Hutchinson file."

Edna was quiet for a long moment, too long.

"Edna, talk," Max insisted.

"You would have terminated an employee for that," she admitted.

Max frowned as much at her words as the itch beneath his cast. "It sounds as if you worked for a tyrannical S.O.B." That she was silent spoke volumes. He scowled as he wandered into the den to his desk. "Was I that bad?"

"You could be demanding. But, Mr. Montgomery—"

"Edna, I asked." From a desk drawer, Max pulled a straightened coat hanger that he'd stashed there days ago. "Don't be concerned about being honest. It's okay." Determined, he slid the wire inside the cast. "I'll talk to you tomorrow." With a quick goodbye to her, he concentrated on the task at hand and worked the wire down to the itch. It was then that he saw Samantha standing in the doorway. "Did you overhear?"

"I heard." She came closer and pointed at the wire. "If you keep doing that, you'll lose good conduct merits, Montgomery."

"It itches like hell." Max removed the wire and stuck it back in the desk drawer.

Sam merely shook her head. "I'm deaf to your complaints."

"You're a hard-hearted woman, Carter."

"Damn straight." She opened the drawer, and for good measure, she took the wire with her. Interested in the photographs, she ambled to the coffee table and flipped open one of the photo albums. "Is this you?" she asked about a photograph of a young boy around seven.

"A lot of the photos are of us as children." Max sidled close and turned a page of the album.

Peering over his shoulder, Sam noted another photo of him when he was around twelve. He looked more sober then. The candid shots that followed were adorable. Two little girls with their dolls were having a tea party under a giant willow tree. A boy in a military school uniform scowled at the camera.

Max turned about ten pages. "These are later ones."

They were of teen years, Sam noted.

"Rachel said that was at a summer formal."

Though younger, Max was just as handsome. Sam viewed the people he'd called friends. An impression of wealth existed. The blond girl with him was sweet, but classic-looking, polished, sophisticated, every hair in place. "Who's the girl?"

"Paige Canterford. Her brother Trey and I were good friends at one time."

Sam stared longer at the girl's photo. Paige suited

him. With some people, breeding carried importance. Ellis would expect his only son to find a woman who'd promote the right image, wouldn't he?

"Did she say if you ever saw him recently?"

Max shook his head. "They moved away."

Once again Sam scrutinized the photographs in the leather-bound album. "And his sister?"

"We weren't serious about each other."

Sam had always known there were blank chapters in his life. It seemed unlikely that a rich, handsome man had never been seriously involved with a woman. But she assumed Paige Canterford hadn't been *the* one. "Want to do something different?"

Max shut the book and set it down. He was more interested in now and the woman near him than a trek down memory lane. "Different, like what?"

Invitingly she swayed toward him, lacing her fingers with his. "Where's your spirit of adventure, Max?" She tugged on his hand to make him move with her.

"Where are we going?" Devilment flashed in his eyes. "Upstairs?"

"For a walk." Sam stifled a snicker as he leveled a scowl at her.

"Where's *your* spirit of adventure?"

"Talk to me later," Sam said with a promise in her voice.

Nine

His arm around her waist now, Max tugged her closer. "A walk wasn't what I had in mind."

"I know. You've already made yourself clear about that. But a walk will be good for you."

He pulled a face. "You're being Florence Nightingale now."

Sam stepped back to place a palm on his back, then nudged him toward the door. "I'm looking out for your welfare."

Over his shoulder, he grinned at her. In the eyes meeting hers, she saw an affectionate look that was far more disturbing than a seductive one. "If you really cared about my—"

"Quit grumbling," Sam insisted as she snagged her sunglasses from the foyer table. "Tell me about the photographs you looked at." She postponed their conversation until she'd closed the door. "Did any of them help?"

A seriousness clouded his eyes. "Not at all."

She wanted to offer encouragement, but doubted anything she said would help. Still, she tried. "When you're ready, you'll remember."

As if it were the most natural thing in the world, he took her hand. "You know, I thought you'd come up with a better idea than taking a walk."

Sam peered over the rim of her sunglasses at him. "Ever play strip poker?"

Dramatically he tapped his fingers at his chest in the vicinity of his heart. "Carter, you take my breath away."

As he dropped his hand to his side, she relaced her fingers with his. "Let's go this way."

"Why? What are you planning?"

Here goes, Sam mused. "I thought we'd visit the Crowleys."

"I gave up strip poker to play Good Neighbor Sam?"

"There's a time for everything."

"You have a torturous nature," he returned.

Enjoying the lighthearted moment, Sam continued the banter. "Am I supposed to feel sorry for you?"

"You're supposed to make me feel better."

"Oh, what a line." As they trudged over a ridge, the Crowleys' home came into view. It was a ranch-style with numerous additions, as if the couple had started small and kept building onto the house.

"The husband doesn't like me," Max seemed compelled to remind her.

Sam reasoned that Joe simply needed to spend time with the new Max. "He will."

"If the purpose of this visit is to find me a bosom buddy—"

How telling his words were. Even with amnesia, he needed a reason for everything. "Sheba is the reason."

"And Sheba is?"

"Their dog. A collie." Sunlight bathed her face with a warm glow. "She had puppies. I'd like to see them."

"Fine. Then you go."

"Cooperate, will you?" Sam noted a stubborn set to his jaw. "Anyway, it's too late to walk away." She directed his stare to the couple approaching them. "Here come Joe and Barbara."

Though Barbara hurried to greet them, Joe lollygagged behind his wife. "What a nice surprise." Barbara hooked her arm in Sam's. "Isn't it, Joe?" she said to her husband who'd finally caught up to her.

"It's a surprise, all right," he mumbled.

"We wanted to see the puppies." Sam hoped the visit went well, hoped to break down the unfriendliness between Max and his neighbors before his amnesia lifted.

Nearing the front door with Barbara, Sam noticed several clocks piled on a table as if left there and forgotten. She paused to examine what looked like an oak gingerbread kitchen clock.

Barbara huffed. "That's my husband's junk collection. He picked those up at a garage sale about three weeks ago. And here they still are."

"They're not junk," Joe protested.

Stopped, Max touched the curved scroll top of one clock. "They sure aren't. This is a pillar-and-scroll clock."

Sam swung around. For a brief second Max's gaze flew to her. She saw his bafflement. Was he wondering, too, how he remembered that?

Joe's chest puffed slightly. "Told you, Barbara. Here's a man who has good taste." He placed a hand on Max's shoulder as if they were old buddies.

Sam shared an I-don't-know-what's-happening-here glance with Barbara.

"Do you collect?" Joe asked.

"No." Max lifted another clock, turned it over. "My grandmother did." He showed no outward reaction, but Sam was sure he was wondering about the sudden memory. "I have her Victorian shelf clock."

"I'd like to see that clock you have," Joe said.

To his credit, Max gave the right response. "Come over sometime."

"We'd like that. And the two of you need to come to our barbecue. It's next week."

Sam swiveled a quick look at Max and nodded her head, prodding him to accept.

"Sure, okay," Max agreed.

Amazing, Sam mused. She couldn't have orchestrated better results, but she wondered if Max had chosen the easiest path, or was warming to his neighbors.

Barbara beamed at both of them. "Wonderful. Now come with me," she urged Sam. "The puppies are outside in back. Some of them look like the father, a Border collie."

Trailing her, Sam whispered in Max's ear, "You need one."

"I don't need one," he murmured back.

"Aw." Sam gushed the moment she stepped outside and spotted the puppies. It was impossible to decide which one was cuter. Several were tan and white like their mother, one of them had a white mask with a black nose, and another had a black face and black saddle but the tip of his tail was white. Another had one ear up and one still drooping. "He's so cute." She bent and picked it up. Petting the small head, she faced Max while the puppies romped around their feet. "Aren't they adorable?"

"Do you want one?" Barbara asked.

"I wish I could. But I live in an apartment. It wouldn't be fair to the dog. And I don't have time."

"If you want one badly enough, you'll make time," Max said.

She assumed that no-nonsense tone belonged to the Max he'd been. She really didn't have time, but he did. Out of the corner of her eye, she noticed he hadn't looked away from the puppy in her arms. If she'd just seen a glimpse of the man known with affection by his sister as "Max the Impossible," then traces of the boy who loved animals must still exist, too. Facing Max, she transferred the puppy to his arm before he could protest.

As if suddenly secure and content, the puppy nuzzled its nose into Max's shirt pocket.

"Max, why don't you—"

"Why don't you?" he countered, and thrust the pup back at her.

Sometimes he truly baffled her, she decided. Why wasn't he grabbing at the opportunity to bring a dog into his life if he always wanted one? "I'll take him," Sam announced. She believed once the puppy lived with him that Max would grow to love it.

"It's yours, not mine," Max reminded her.

Sam nodded agreeably, but she believed differently. Max was wrong, of course. With the puppy in her arms, she stroked its soft fur and walked with Max back toward the house. She recalled how the puppy had snuggled into him. This was his dog—only he didn't know it yet.

While Max wandered into his den, she found a cardboard box for the dog, and retrieved the morning newspaper from the trash can to line the box. When the puppy plopped down to sleep, she started dinner.

The sound of Sam's laughter, and the mouthwatering aromas drifting to him from the kitchen, enticed Max from the den half an hour later. At the kitchen doorway, he heard her talking. From the conversation, he gathered she was on the phone with Jessica McCallum.

Her back to him, she chatted away about the puppy. "It's just adorable, Jessica."

Awake and whimpering, the puppy had conned her with doleful-looking eyes and managed an escape from the box. As it wandered from one corner of the kitchen to another, Max wondered if it was getting ready to mark its spot.

Stirring something in a pot on the stove, Sam went on. "I haven't thought of a name yet. I hope Max will help name him."

Max scowled at the pup sniffing around his shoe. He had no intentions of getting involved with it. Intending to put the pup back in its box, he bent and picked it up. Okay, it was cute, he admitted to himself. But it might be because of his amnesia that he was feeling such softness for the round ball of fur curled in his arm.

He'd resisted bringing it home for good reason. Sure he'd want it now, but what about later? Could he trust any feelings he had now? He even had to wonder about ones for Sam. He wasn't certain it had been fair to get involved with her. Hell of a time to think about that, he mused.

But he didn't know the man everyone told him he'd been. From what he'd learned, the person Sam had begun to care about wasn't the real Max Montgomery. When his memory came back, would he feel the same desperation to hold her in his arms? Would her lips taste as sweet to him? Would he yearn for moments like this, for the sound of her voice? Max set the puppy down and watched it scamper toward Sam.

In response, she crouched and lifted it to her to kiss the top of its head. "Scruffy?" Sam made a face. "I don't think that name would work for him, Jessica. 'Scruffy' sounds small and cutesy. Oh, sure the puppy is cute. But one day it might be a majestic-looking dog." Her laughter rippled out at something Jessica said.

Max stayed out of her view. Clearly she'd made some good friends since coming to Whitehorn five years ago. He'd lived in the town most of his life and had few.

"Max? Max?" her voice sang out, assuring him that she'd repeated the question since ending her phone call. "Where are you?"

He focused and grinned at her. "It smells great in here."

Pleasure rushed color into her face. "Thank you." Having set the puppy down, she went to the sink and washed her hands. "You keep saying things like that and I'll change professions."

He doubted that. He moseyed near as she took the meat from the pan. He'd been with her long enough to sense she was the dedicated type. Without hovering, she'd kept a close eye on him during the first days he was home. She'd handled small jobs like cutting food for him, yet given him room to keep his independence. She was an excellent nurse. Though her sunny disposition had annoyed him at times, it had also forced his spirits up.

"Seriously, I love to cook, and bake," she said. "A German lady I nursed made desserts to die for."

While she dished potatoes onto a plate, he paused

behind her. "She must have taught you well. You're no slouch at making them."

Over her shoulder, she grinned at him. "I'm no slouch at lots of things."

He pushed her hair to the side. With her soft pale skin bewitching him, he lost himself in her scent and kissed the nape of her neck. "After last night, I'd never argue."

They were nearly done with dinner when company arrived. Looking past Sam toward the window, Max regarded the white pickup parking in his driveway. "Who's that?"

Sam raised her gaze from her plate. "The Kincaids. That's Garrett and Collin Kincaid." She stood, then skirted the table to cross toward the door.

Max wasn't sure he wanted visitors, but she was already inviting them in. Decades separated the ages of the men. They had similar blue eyes and handsome looks. One was silver-haired. The other was dark-haired, around Max's age, and nearly as tall.

"We came to visit," the older man said with a step inside. "Hope we're not disturbing your dinner."

Sam shook her head. "No, no. We're done."

Garrett smiled at her, then swung questioning eyes on Max. "I heard you might not remember us."

Max hated this, truly hated this. "I don't."

As Max stood, the older man offered his hand. "Garrett Kincaid."

From others, Max had heard about Garrett Kincaid.

In his seventies, the man was the patriarch of the Kincaids, and a fair and honest man.

"Collin Kincaid," the other man said as they exchanged a handshake. "Garrett is my grandfather."

With the introductions done, Max ushered them toward the den doorway. Was this just a social visit, or had they come expecting something from him? Every time someone came to see him, he questioned what the person wanted.

"We wondered if you were doing better." The older man settled on the settee. "The doctors said everything will come back to you, didn't they?"

Repeatedly, Max mused. But when? "That's what they said." Max watched Sam bring in their coffee and set down the tray. He mouthed a thank-you to her. She did a lot of jobs that were above and beyond what she was hired for.

As she breezed out of the room, Collin cleared his throat. "We meant to come sooner." Annoyance danced across his face as his beeper went off.

Garrett whipped a glare in his grandson's direction. "Who?" he asked simply.

Head bent, Collin squinted at the number on his beeper. "The lawyer."

Irritation deepened the frown lines on Garrett's face. "You know about our problem, don't you?" he asked Max. "Hell, of course, you probably don't. I keep forgetting that you don't remember any of this."

Rather than insensitive, the man came across as blunt. He'd said what was the truth. What could Max say to counter him? He'd get flashes of memories, but most of the time he was like a person who entered the theater too late for the start of the movie, and didn't know who the players were. "I've heard," Max answered. "My father mentioned it."

Garrett offered his own version of the problem with Jordon Baxter and the land they were fighting over.

"It'll be a battle," Collin admitted. He set down his empty coffee cup. "Why we really came was to let you know that we're near if you need anything." When Collin stood, Max rose and touched his shoulder. "Thanks. Come again, will you?"

Collin stopped and smiled slightly. He actually appeared stumped by something. "Is this the new-and-improved Max Montgomery?"

Was he so different? "I guess so." People reacted as if he was acting odd. From what he'd previously been told about himself, it had to be an improvement.

He walked the Kincaids to the door and watched their truck pull away. Before he could walk back to the den, Merv Talbot arrived. "Told you I'd be back."

Max couldn't say he was thrilled but wanted to get to know the man better. "Would you like a drink?"

"No." Merv glanced at his watch. "I can't stay long. But I wanted to check on you."

"Why?"

"We used to be best friends, Max."

Max asked the logical question. "Why 'used to be'?"

"It was a long time ago when we were real close. Before you went to college."

Max didn't understand. Here was a part of his past with no clear-cut answers. Why would he distance himself from a friend? "What went wrong between us? Did something happen in college? Did we go to the same one?"

Merv chuckled good-naturedly. "You were the studious one, Max, not me. But you were okay the first semester. During the second year, you changed. You didn't want to see any of us. You said that you were busy. You wanted to concentrate on your career."

None of this made sense to Max. Was he always so self-centered? "And nothing else mattered?"

"You were single-minded. When you wanted something, nothing stopped you from going after it." Merv's attention shifted to his watch. "Damn, it's later than I thought. How about lunch next week?"

"I'll call you."

Was there more left unsaid? Max wondered. Was Merv doling out bits and pieces of information because of his amnesia? "Be straight with me. Did something happen?"

Merv held out a hand, palm up. "Max, I honestly don't know. There was a woman. I gather that you were in love with her. I'm not sure. I never met her. All I knew about her was her name."

In love with her? How could he have loved some woman and not even remember who she was, what she looked like? "What was her name?"

"Michelle."

Frustration swarmed in on him. Damn it, why

couldn't he remember people? Tense now, he saw Merv to the door, said goodbye, then returned to the den. What had happened in college that had changed him? Was it about some woman named Michelle? Who the hell was she?

"You look troubled."

Max whipped around toward Sam's voice. Confused by unanswered questions, he needed her, her softness and strength at the moment. He'd become too close to her to pretend nothing was wrong.

She stepped near and placed her palms on his chest. "Did the Kincaids tell you about their problem?" she asked because she could think of no other reason for the look on his face.

"Do you know about it?"

"I know Garrett Kincaid is still looking for his seventh illegitimate grandson," Sam answered. "And that he's trying to settle the dispute over the land with Jordan Baxter so he can give his grandsons what he thinks they deserve."

"Through their lawyers, they plan to set up a meeting with this guy Baxter."

"I doubt he'll agree," Sam said. "Jordan Baxter tells anyone who'll listen that the Kincaids are trying to steal his ranch from him."

This was the worst part of not remembering, Max thought. He hated his inability to recall small details in his life. "Who is Baxter?"

"A local businessman. He deals in real estate mostly. He's not liked, and for good reason. He's closed down shopkeepers who didn't meet his rent increases. He's evicted tenants because they're living in properties he wants to dump." Sam paused and searched his face, trying to decipher if his mood had lifted any. She saw no smile in his eyes. "And now Baxter insists he found some lost letter that willed him the land."

"It's clear Garrett won't be deterred," Max told her. "He plans to buy the land, insists his grandchildren deserve their fair share."

"Something is bothering you."

She'd become his companion, his friend, his sounding board, his lover. He felt at ease sharing anything with her. "After they left, Merv Talbot came." A sense of the man he'd been had grown stronger while he'd been with Merv again. A friend meant camaraderie, laughs, trust. To find someone he'd shared all that with had made him feel less lost. But even that friendship wasn't solid.

Repeatedly he was forced to face the man he'd been, someone who was hard on employees, ruthlessly practical in business, unaffectionate with family and estranged from a friend. Why? Did a woman named Michelle hold the key or was she someone else he'd pushed away?

Michelle… Merv had acted as if the woman had changed him.

Totally confused, he'd stepped closer when Merv had turned to leave. Max had wanted to grab him, stop him. *Tell me more,* he wanted to shout. *Damn it, fill in the empty places.* "Thanks for telling me that much," he'd said instead. But he'd been floundering. The name had meant nothing to him.

"Max?" Sam's gaze had darkened with interest.

"Merv said there was a woman when I was in college." A need to touch her overwhelming him, he tucked strands of her hair behind her ear. "Her name was Michelle. He didn't know anything else. From someone, I need to learn about her."

"Then we will," she said with a certainty that made him believe she was right.

Another woman would have wanted to know more. Was Michelle that important to him, someone he had loved? "No questions?"

"Why should there be?"

She gave and gave, and never took. Gently he caught her at the curve of her waist and brought her closer so he felt the heat of her against him. "Want to do something?"

A teasing lightness warmed her voice. "Something specific?"

Max buried his face in her hair. "You could say that."

Ten

She was an angel, his rescuer, his lifeline to sanity.

Her sultry laugh slithered over him. "Think we can make it up those steps this time?"

They kissed, took a few steps, kissed again. He needed some kind of identification, real and tangible. For a while he could find that with her, as her lover.

By the time they reached the bedroom, he was aching for her, longing to make her breathless, make her shudder. Standing in front of him, beside the bed, she stepped back and pulled the shirt up and over her head. With her scent floating over him, Max lowered his mouth to the lacy trim of her bra, to the swell of her breast above it.

Her scent was there, soft and subtle, enticing. Desire coiled tighter within him as the wispy cloth fell away.

He closed his mouth over the soft roundness, licked at the erect and hard nipple.

Longing heated his blood. Hearing her murmur his name, he shifted to slip fingers into her jeans, her panties. Pleasing her was his only thought. "You're so soft," he whispered when his hand made contact with the delicate, sensitive skin. Against him, he felt her tremble. He wanted to give this time. He wanted to cover her, press down on her, fill her. He wanted to do more than he was able, and he damned the cast as he yearned to move both hands over her.

Instead she unfastened buttons, she pulled down zippers. Her eyes never leaving his, she stripped clothing from them.

He'd give her more. One day he'd make her mindless as he'd toy with buttons, inch clothes from her. One day, he promised, dragging her closer, his mouth on hers again. He curved her into him when they sank to the mattress. He wanted to pleasure her. He wanted a slow pace. But as she moved back, as he stared at the crown of her head, as the heat of her breath closed over him, he couldn't speak. He was lost to everything else. He pushed his head back, unable to think. All his senses centered on the warmth of her breath on his skin. With a touch, a caress, she rendered him helpless.

He groaned her name. She was driving him mad, giving him strength—weakening him. Eyes squeezed tight, he clutched onto a shred of control. Desire licked at him like fire. Blood pounded through his head.

Aching, he tempered his hunger to stretch out the moment. But with the final pleasure almost upon him, he gave up.

Breathing hard, he stared up at her as she shifted, wanting to see her eyes. Fiery-red hair framed her face, and passion softened her eyes. She straddled him, and without a word spoken, as if they were one, her body opened to welcome him.

The heat closed and tightened around him, and all the desire for her rushed him. Slowly she began to move, at first alone, then as one with him. And she rode him until his breath was ragged, until he felt consumed by the need to fill her. Eyes closed, his heart thundering, he knew without doubt that he would have journeyed wherever she led.

Sam had no idea when she'd fallen asleep, but as with last night, contentment cocooned her the next morning. Cuddling against Max, she stared at the bedroom ceiling cast in the gray light of dawn. *Closeness.* He might not understand his need for it, but she resolved to have it with him. A closeness that went beyond intimacy. Recently he'd begun to trust her with his thoughts, his feelings.

Nothing was easy for him, neither the loss of memories nor the vague, incomplete recollections. And as she longed to be a part of his pain and joy, she wanted to share not only her body but also feelings with him. Angling her face toward his, she was unexpectedly rewarded with a kiss. "Good morning."

"Want something?" he murmured against her hair.

"More of that." He kissed her again. I need you to love me, she wanted to say to him even as she tried to remember that these moments might be all they'd have.

Again she rested her head on his shoulder. How would she ever walk away from him? Life would go on, but she knew she would be changed. Tenderly she ran a fingertip along his rib cage. She'd found love. A person changed when it was lost.

"Hear that?"

When he groaned, she laughed. From downstairs came a high-pitched howl. Definitely the puppy planned to not be forgotten. His yipping grew louder, more demanding, more woeful.

"Tell me this isn't going to go on all the time," Max grumbled.

"He's probably scared." No way could she ignore the puppy's yipping. "I left a light on, but this was his first night away from the others. I'll go downstairs."

Max merely grunted, turning his face into his pillow.

"Now what drawer had those old socks in it?" she said more to herself than him.

"My socks?" He rolled from his side onto his back, and peered at her. "Why *my* socks?"

Sam scrambled from the bed to his dresser and opened a drawer. "Puppies calm down if they have something with their owner's scent on it."

"Then give him *your* sock."

She rummaged through the rolled socks for one with material thinning at the heel. "I only have a few with me." The quickly gathered excuse made sense to her.

"You shouldn't give him a sock." His words came out muffled as he resumed his love affair with his pillow. "It's a bad habit to start."

"Is it?" A sock dangling from her fingers, Sam shrugged into his terry-cloth robe. "How do you know that?"

"I just know," he mumbled.

Starting for the door, she rolled up the overlong sleeves into bulky cuffs. "I'll get a book on dog care later. For now, emergency treatment is a necessity." When she opened the bedroom door, a high, squealing howl drifted through the downstairs rooms and up the steps to her.

Behind her, Max moaned.

Amused, Sam cast a look over her shoulder to see him bury his head beneath his pillow. "Definitely an emergency."

"If you need help, don't call."

She smiled to herself and left the room. She recalled him holding the puppy the night before and petting it. Mr. Tough Guy had succumbed to the puppy's charm more than once.

Halfway down the stairs, Sam slowed her pace, aware the puppy's whining had suddenly stopped. She noticed something else, too. Reaching the foot of the staircase, she inhaled deeply, took in the wonderful smells wafting on the air.

The new cook had arrived, it seemed, and while

Sam loved to cook, she never minded the treat of eating someone else's cooking.

Intrigued by the smell of bacon, she wandered into the room. Standing at the stove, the cook, an ample-figured, tall woman with a lopsided bun, raised her eyes from a bowl of pancake batter. "Good morning, miss."

"Good morning." Sam introduced herself, and within minutes she was laughing with Josie, a gregarious and forthright woman.

"I started breakfast, then let the puppy out. Was that okay with you?" she asked.

"It was nice of you to do that." After Max had fallen asleep last night, Sam had peeked in from the kitchen door to see the whimpering puppy sitting with its rump halfway in the dish of water she'd left him. The water had been dumped, a puddle staining the newspaper. She'd leaned over the makeshift pen of chicken wire that she'd found in the garage and had gathered the dog to her. His whining had stopped immediately. In her arms, he'd yawned, then had nuzzled closer and gone to sleep.

Now, happy with company around him, he chased a small, rubber ball that Sam had found in a kitchen drawer before leaving him, a surprise for when he woke up.

"I just love dogs. Now, he's a real cute one, isn't he?" Josie, it seemed, was as much a sucker for dogs as she was.

Sam squatted beside the pup and scratched behind

its ear. "The neighbors gave me a small bag of food until I could get to the store."

"If you want, I'll pick something up." Josie poured pancake batter into a pan. "I need to buy a few things for meals."

Sam's gaze shifted to the doorway and a smiling Max.

"I smell coffee."

His eyes stayed on her, warming her. If desire was all she felt for him, how simple this time with him might have been. Enjoy the moment, treasure the memory and move on. That used to be her way. But not this time. This time she yearned for more—everything.

"I'm Josie," the cook was saying. She wiped her hand on her apron and stepped forward.

Max took her hand. "Nice to meet you, Josie. My sister claims you have excellent references."

She grinned wide. "Thank you, sir. Would you like coffee?"

"I'd love a cup."

Her jaw dropped as Max sat on a chair at the kitchen table. "Here, sir?"

"Right here." Max shared an amused exchange with Sam. "So how's what's-his-name doing?"

Sam assumed he meant the puppy. "He's getting used to his new home. He needs a name. Give him one."

As if warding off evil, he held up a hand. "Not me. You name him."

Sam sighed, wishing she could shake some good

sense into him. A firm connection to the puppy would be good for him. Pets worked wonders at healing invisible wounds.

"Last time I had a dog was when my daughter and I lived in Seattle," Josie said. "I'm glad you have one, sir."

Max didn't bother to argue with the hefty Amazon who'd taken over his kitchen. "Love them."

"I knew we'd get along. I never believe gossip."

In the way of people aware of each other's thoughts, Max exchanged a look with Sam. He assumed she was thinking what he was. As she had, he refrained from asking Josie what she meant. Apparently she'd heard tales about the man who'd existed before the accident.

"Breakfast is ready," she announced brightly, carrying a platter of food as if she was about to show off the Hope diamond.

The pancakes with blueberries were delicious and filling. "These are wonderful, aren't they?" Sam poked her fork into another morsel.

Over the rim of his cup, he grinned at her. "They're good."

Sam laughed at his understated response. He'd eaten more than his fair share.

"But I can think of something that might be better," he said low.

No mind-reading ability was needed to guess what he meant. A teasing light shone in his eyes. "I love the way you think."

In comfortable silence, they finished a last cup of coffee. Through the screen door, a warm breeze flowed in. In nearby trees, several birds serenaded them. Everything seemed perfect to her. If only it could last.

Setting down her empty cup, she considered suggesting a drive. But he looked suddenly preoccupied as if something weighty was on his mind. "You're off somewhere again."

He grinned wryly, indicating his thoughts weren't intense. "I was thinking about Rachel. What's the story about Alyssa being found? You said something about some woman named Cobbs. Who is she?"

"Winona Cobbs," Sam told him. "After Christina was found—" She paused. It seemed so insensitive to blurt the word "dead." "Well...police believed the baby wasn't alive. But Winona Cobbs assured Rachel that the baby was well."

"That's what I thought you'd said." His fingers moved near her hand resting on the table, stroked the top of her knuckles. "She's a psychic?"

"She's a character," Sam said lightly. "She also runs a junkyard. I know it sounds ridiculous to rely on what she said—"

"She sounds like a kook."

She'd expected his skepticism. "Whether she is or not, she was right about Alyssa."

Stuffed from too many pancakes, Sam left him and wandered to her room to dress. While she wiggled into jeans, she swore not to overindulge daily on Josie's fantastic culinary treats or she'd turn into a blimp.

With the puppy in her arms, she joined Max on the patio. To keep an eye on the pup, she sat on the grass. "Did you know there's a country music concert a few nights from now in Bozeman?"

Sitting on a nearby patio chair, he set down his newspaper. "Is that important to you?"

Sam saw amusement in his eyes. That he thought she was hinting for a night out stirred her laugh. "No, not to me. Rachel wanted to go. She was thrilled when she and Jack got tickets." Sam relayed a previous phone conversation she'd had with his sister. "But then she learned that Lesley was going, too. She usually baby-sits for them," she explained. "Your sister's not too big on trusting just anyone to sit with Alyssa. So I suggested we baby-sit."

Max arched a brow.

Though he'd never actually said to her that he wanted to spend more time with Alyssa, Sam had seen during Rachel's and Alyssa's last visit that he'd kept his gaze fixed on the little one. Perhaps he was looking for some resemblance to Christina. "Was I wrong?" She loved babies, kids of any age. "If you don't want to—"

"I do."

Sam started to smile, then stopped. For the briefest second, a vacant look returned to his eyes, then he blinked and focused on her. She made a logical guess about where his mind had wandered. "Who will you ask about that woman—Michelle?"

"Rachel," he said simply. "If she doesn't have

answers, I don't know who to ask. From what Merv said, she was important to me."

Sam viewed his answer as progress. At some moment, he'd begun to trust his sister.

"Someone should know something about her. Merv told me that I'd loved her." A trace of what sounded like disgust and frustration colored his voice. "I loved her but I can't even remember what she looked like."

With a look away, Sam inhaled a hard breath. She'd always known there must be a special woman. A woman from Max's past. Now she had to question if that woman would be part of his future, too. Would he realize he still loved her? Was she the one who'd be like this with him once he got his memory back?

"Hello," a feminine voice rang out.

Sam snapped a look at the doorway and saw Rachel.

Blossoming with her pregnancy, Rachel manipulated her way through the terrace doors with a sleeping Alyssa in her arms and an oversize diaper bag hanging from a shoulder. In passing, she affectionately patted Max's cheek.

As though she'd made him aware he needed a shave, Max ran a hand over the stubble on his jaw. "Why isn't she ever awake?" he said about Alyssa.

"I'll come by later next time." She dropped the diaper bag to the flagstone floor, then placed Alyssa on the nearby chaise longue. "I wanted to see if the new cook had arrived." She sniffed at the air. "What is that she's cooking?" She plopped onto the closest chair and smoothed the material of her maternity top over her rounded belly.

She glows, Sam thought. "Smells wonderful, doesn't it? Josie is making crab cakes for lunch. Want to join us?"

"I wish I could. But Alyssa has a doctor's appointment. O-oh." Rachel's expression turned mushy as she spotted the puppy. "What have you got?"

"Max has a puppy," Sam piped in. If she said it often enough, she believed that he'd stop resisting the idea.

"*You* have a puppy," he countered.

She added stubbornness to his personality traits.

Rachel laughed. "So why did you get one?" she asked Max to Sam's delight.

"I didn't." He pointed at Sam. "She did."

"He's so adorable."

Sam joined forces with Rachel to ignore Max's protest and steered the conversation in another direction. "I imagine you're looking forward to having the baby soon."

Rachel's face shone with happiness. "It's only a few months, but I feel as if it's taking forever. Jack can hardly wait, too," she admitted. "Having Alyssa has made us aware of how much we wanted a family. And we think of her as our own."

"She is now, isn't she?" Max questioned.

Dread crept into his sister's darkened eyes. "Not really. Alyssa's real father is near. The note he left indicated that he would be back for her. I've always known that might happen."

Rachel's attempt to seem accepting of the fact fell flat. Anyone who saw the love in her eyes when she cared for Alyssa could surmise that a separation from the baby would be devastating for her.

"Who's Alyssa's doctor?" Sam asked.

"Dr. Carey Hall."

"Dr. Carey Hall Kincaid?" Sam asked to verify. "She's a wonderful pediatrician."

Rachel nodded. "Sometimes I forget. I'm so used to calling her Dr. Hall. She's married to Wayne Kincaid," she explained, seeing Max's frown.

"I don't know them." Max gave a self-deprecating laugh. "But that's not unusual. I don't know a lot of people. Collin and Garrett Kincaid came by yesterday," he informed her.

Delight brightened Rachel's eyes. "That's wonderful." Her voice trailed off, along with her pleasure when she noted the grim set of Max's mouth. "Or wasn't it?" She regarded him at length. "You look less than pleased."

"It was okay. After they left, Merv Talbot came."

"Merv and you used to be good friends," Rachel said.

"So he said. He mentioned a woman named Michelle. Do you know about her?"

Rachel appeared bewildered. "Michelle?" In what appeared to be avoidance, she dodged his stare and wandered over to check on Alyssa. "Max, I don't think—"

"Rachel." An appeal crept into his voice. "If you know something, tell me."

Rachel's blue eyes flew to Sam with a plea for help. Sam believed Max needed answers to any questions he asked. It was the only means for him to work his way back.

Conflicting emotions crossed his sister's face. Clearly she was caught between her innate honesty and a desire to shield him from something. "We were told that too much, too quickly wouldn't be good for you, Max."

"Neither is this emptiness in my mind." Max understood her attempt to protect him but didn't like it. "Merv said I knew her in college."

"Yes. You cared about her," Rachel confirmed.

"Merv said 'loved,'" Max countered to gauge her reaction.

"I don't know if— Yes," she admitted. "I think you did for a short time."

Why not any longer? Tired of the questions in his mind, he relied on Rachel to answer the most important one. "Where is she now?"

"I'm not sure." Rachel dropped into a chair near him. "She was in San Diego."

"Go on," he insisted. "I need to know what you know, Rachel. What happened with her?"

Concern etched into her face. "You two had gone out to eat." She heaved a breath. "There was an accident. It was snowing, and the car skidded."

Max tensed. A car accident. He thought this might be about some woman he'd jilted or who'd dumped him. "Was she hurt?"

Rachel spoke softly. "Max, she recovered."

Breathing seemed more difficult for him suddenly. He sensed it hadn't been a fender-bender. *Don't jump to conclusions. Ask questions.* "Recovered from what? How badly was she hurt?"

Her silence spoke volumes. Whatever she wasn't saying was bad.

"Rachel?"

"She was paralyzed."

His stomach clenched. Was. She'd said "was," he reminded himself. "Is she still?"

In a reassuring gesture, she stretched toward him, touched his hand. "No, she isn't. Doctors didn't think she'd walk, but she did, Max."

He pulled his hand free of hers. "A miracle?"

Silent, watching and listening, Sam rode on his emotions. He sounded so cynical suddenly that her heart ached for him.

He stood, said nothing, moved away from them to the edge of the patio.

Rachel hurried the words. "Max, she went through months of rehabilitation, but she got better."

"Who ended it?" He looked paler when he faced them. "Did she not want to see me ever again? Or did I—"

"Stop," Rachel insisted as if sensing the blame he was placing on himself. "You did everything you could. After the accident, you were with her every day at the hospital. You didn't shirk responsibility, Max. You weren't that kind of man."

"So who ended the relationship?"

"She—she did. She fell in love with a doctor."

And broke his heart? Sam wondered. Or had he been ready for the relationship to end? She studied Rachel, trying to understand what hadn't been said, why Rachel had sounded so desperate to make Max listen to her.

But he wasn't listening. He'd already swung away.

"Max," Rachel called after him.

Worry for him skittered through Sam, too, as he started down the grassy incline behind the house. What was it that his sister hadn't said?

"I really thought he didn't need to know all that."

Years of being more invisible than a book on a shelf while she was working for people gave Sam some insight. She'd witnessed the look in a person's eyes when with good intentions they held back information. Had he suffered some injury that had a bearing on his health now? That seemed unlikely. As his private nurse, Sam would have been informed about it. Still she asked, "He was okay? Not hurt?"

"Yes, thank God." With some effort, Rachel pushed to her feet. "Sam, thank you."

Sam stood, too. "For what?"

"For caring so much about my brother. You love him, don't you?"

"Rachel, I'm his—"

Rachel raised a silencing hand. "Don't try to pretend with me." Rachel laid a hand on her shoulder. "He needs you, Samantha."

And I need him. Anything else Rachel wanted to say remained unsaid as Max reappeared at the top of the hill. Not wanting to upset him more, before he came near, Sam steered conversation toward their baby-sitting job, told Rachel they'd sit with Alyssa. "So what time will you be bringing her?" she asked.

"We'll drop off Alyssa around six-thirty." Rachel waited for her brother to come near. "Are you all right?"

Sam believed he would lie rather than cause his sister more worry.

"I'm fine." Affectionately he cupped a hand over her shoulder and kissed her cheek. "Thanks for telling me."

"Understand that Michelle is happy now," Rachel pointed out.

His face grew stony, his eyes shuttered. "We'll see you," he said instead of responding.

Concerned for him, too, Sam refused to let him lock her out and go off somewhere alone. "Are you really fine?" she asked after Rachel had gone.

He faced her squarely. "I can't even remember the face of the woman I sent to the hospital."

Sam heard a trace of blame in his voice. "Your sister said it was an accident. Remember that, Max."

An uneasiness washed over him. Max couldn't pinpoint what caused it. He assumed it was a reaction to a vague memory of the accident, of a woman's pain.

But he was relieved to know that he hadn't dumped the woman after learning she was paralyzed. He'd hate to think that when faced with a difficult situation he'd taken off. It seemed he had some redeemable qualities. He stared at Sam, and hoped she thought so, too.

Eleven

Over the next two days neither of them mentioned Michelle again. Sam assumed Max considered the woman a part of his past. Whatever feelings he harbored about her and that tragic night remained masked behind his amnesia.

Sam yawned, trying to play catch-up after an exhausting day yesterday. She and Max had spent a fun time at a local fair, walking around exhibits, and later had joined a crowd on the bleachers and watched a rodeo. In the evening, they'd shared a romantic dinner out, and beneath candlelight and soft music, they'd enjoyed some spicy pasta.

Actually looking forward to a more relaxing evening, she was glad they'd be staying home to baby-sit tonight. The only thing she and Max had to do was drive to town for his doctors' appointments.

When they reached the town's main street, Sam offered a suggestion. "We could go to the bank, to your office, when you're done at the doctor's. Being in familiar places has been known to help."

"That hasn't worked so far," he reminded her.

There were no words to make this easier on him. No one knew when or if he would ever remember everything. Perhaps he'd simply have to come to terms with his loss of memory. But at least his body was healing.

By his muttered curse after they'd traveled down the town's main street, Sam assumed nothing had triggered memories for him.

Max said as much when they were ambling across the street from the parking lot of Whitehorn Memorial to the doctor's office. "Not a damn thing means anything. Like before when I was here, I can't recall if I ever stepped into any store."

Sam traced his stare to an outdoors outfitters business. "Why do you wonder? Did someone tell you that you like camping and stuff?"

"And stuff," he answered. "Fishing, mostly. Talbot said that I'd planned to go on a fishing trip with him and his brother-in-law." He heaved a deep breath. "I'm so tired of all the guesswork." He touched the back of her neck, halted her with him. He looked for words to tell her how important she'd become to him. "You deserve more. More laughter, more good moments."

Sam heard a weariness in his voice. "I'm not complaining," she assured him.

Lightly he kissed the bridge of her nose. "You've been cheated, you know."

Sam didn't think so. She'd found far more than she'd ever expected. "In what way?"

A smile, faintly strained, curled the edges of his lips upwards. "I've never sent you flowers."

A mood shift, Sam noted. Previously he'd shown a tendency to shift conversation, using humorous words or a tease to pull away from a dark mood. "I like any kind." She felt the stares of a few passersby, didn't care. Looking as if there was no one else in the world, they stood like lovers on the sidewalk in the middle of town. "I always wanted a flower garden."

His gaze held hers. "Why didn't you have one?"

"I live in an apartment, Max." Footsteps behind her made her step back from him. Sam nodded a hello to the town's librarian. "I never lived in a house."

Attuned to each other, at the same moment, they resumed walking. Max's hand closed over hers. "And I never brought you breakfast in bed."

Sam decided that he was acting strange, but went along with him. "You're going to do that?" she asked on a laugh.

"You deserve it."

A lightness had entered his voice. Sam hoped it wasn't forced. "I have a lot to look forward to, don't I?"

At the door to the doctor's office, he discreetly

skimmed the round softness of her hip before reaching for the doorknob. "Whatever you want."

She smiled up at him, wishing that were true.

Because the doctor might have special orders, Sam accompanied Max into the office for the appointment. They entered to find one man in the waiting room.

"We'll set up appointments for your daughters' immunizations on that day then, Mitch," the nurse was saying.

Sam had heard that the woman had been around forever and knew everyone. While Max took a seat and grabbed a magazine, Sam fell in line behind the lean, strong-looking man. With his sandy-brown hair and tanned skin, he looked like a working man, one who made his living outdoors. Sam only knew the widower by name—Mitch Fielding—and his reputation for being an A-1 carpenter and handyman.

Finished making back-to-back appointments, he turned around and delivered a polite, quick grin at Sam, one with the power to kickstart a few feminine hearts. She returned his smile and stepped forward to talk to the nurse.

After he was out of hearing range, she seemed compelled to say, "He has beautiful six-year-old twin girls."

"I've seen them," Sam responded. "They're really cute."

Still smiling, the woman looked down and made a quick notation in the appointment book.

Rachel turned away to see Max setting down the

magazine. He stood as the nurse opened the door that led to the doctor's office.

"The doctor will see you now, Mr. Montgomery."

"You look well, Max," he said as a greeting. In a scrutinizing manner, he peered over the top of his wire-rimmed glasses at him. "Unbelievably rested."

"TLC," Max quipped.

The doctor's pale blue eyes twinkled. "I see. TLC is often the best medicine."

With both of them staring at her suddenly, Sam's face warmed. To her credit, she managed to stifle the blush.

"Seriously, Max, you look quite well."

Sam guessed the word not said. Different. A relaxed, pleasant-looking Max Montgomery had been a rare sight around town. Twice during their walk, acquaintances of Sam's had said hello and Max had responded with a greeting. One man had nearly jerked his head off his neck with his double take. Max had changed, and people were noticing.

"Go slow," the doctor said before they left his office.

"Go slow." Max mumbled with disgust on the way out of the building. "What the hell does he think I've been doing?" Disdainfully he eyed the cast and the blue sling that he still wore.

Sam smiled sweetly. "Grumble, grumble."

He sent her a killing look. "Having fun at my expense?"

Sometimes his disagreeableness bordered on comical. "Immensely."

In answer he caught her at the waist and tugged her against him. Sam released a low husky laugh against his lips. "So abused."

With time to spare before a second doctor's appointment, they headed for the bank.

"You are in trouble, you know," she teased Max. "I couldn't believe you'd said that to the doctor about TLC."

When his eyes locked with hers, she saw the mischief in them. "It's the truth. And you do deserve the credit. You're an excellent nurse. Whenever I needed you, you were there. You knew when to help and when not to, so I would stay independent. That kind of insight comes from experience and from an ability to read people."

"Stop. This praise will go to my head. Much more, and you'll make me blush."

"Again," Max teased her about her reaction in the doctor's office.

"I didn't."

His grin widened. "Did."

Sam saw no point in arguing when he was right. "By the way, thank you. But you have a favorably slanted view because—"

Max crowded her for a second, bringing them so close their hips brushed. "Because you make me senseless?"

Pleasure rushing her, she lovingly touched his cheek as he reached around her to open one of the bank's glass doors. "I hope so."

* * *

The troops came to attention the instant the first teller inside the bank spotted him.

A security guard, a man old enough to be Max's grandfather, scurried over. "It's good to see you, Mr. Montgomery."

Max stilled. Memories. He needed memories. "I'm sorry. I don't remember your name."

Puzzlement pinched a line between the man's gray brows. "Sir, I'm sure you never knew it."

Because he'd never asked, Max assumed. "What is it?"

"Dennison, sir. Fred Dennison."

"It's good to be back, Mr. Dennison."

The man nodded, kept nodding even when Max had started to walk away. In passing, several employees said obligatory hellos. Max didn't miss their surprised looks when he returned the greeting. Had he really been that unfriendly? Rachel had told him that he was known around town as Scrooge, a man with a bad disposition and an ungenerous heart. Charles Dickens. *A Christmas Carol.* Funny he had no problem recalling the book. It was who Max Montgomery was that he couldn't remember.

"Your office is this way," Sam said low, to keep their conversation private.

With her beside him, engineering him past the tellers and down a hallway, he found his office. Every step he took intensified the emotion building within him. What if he never connected to anything from his past? Hell. A panic attack threatened. What if everything was foreign to him? He hated the fear rising within him, wanted to whip around and leave.

The moment he opened the door to the outer office, a friendly face smiled at him. Sitting behind a computer, a telephone cradled between her jaw and shoulder, Edna wagged fingers at them.

Max took a few moments to scan her office while she finished her business call. It was a white room with deep blue accents. Reprints of Monet's work adorned the walls. Had he or some interior decorator chosen them?

"Good morning, Mr. Montgomery."

Max thought Edna sounded pleased to see him.

"As you requested yesterday morning during our phone conversation, I've rescheduled that meeting with the board of directors."

"Thank you, Edna." He glanced in Sam's direction. Patiently she stood near, saying nothing. She wouldn't push. He hadn't been lying about her insight. She knew when to prod, to nudge, and when to give him space to find his own way. Like now. He stared at his office door, just stared. This is stupid, he told himself. Go in.

For the second time in minutes he opened another door, hoping to unlock the one in his mind. The room was somber, respectable-looking, with plush gray carpeting, a muted blue settee and matching chair, and a long, highly polished, cherry desk. A painting, an abstract with its splashes of yellow and orange and blue, was the one touch of bright color.

To see how it felt, Max settled on the forest-green wing chair behind the desk. For a moment he stared out the floor-to-ceiling window with its view of the town's business section. No memory sprang forth. He couldn't recall ever sitting here, ever staring out this window before.

He touched the phone on his desk, the blotter pad, a pen in the desk's center drawer. He opened others, touched papers. Unlike a psychic, he received no images. Disgusted, and with panic teetering close by, he shoved the chair back from the desk and pushed himself to a stand. Coming to the office had been a waste of time.

From the corner of his eye, he saw Sam. She hovered in the doorway as if to give him time with his own thoughts. Why couldn't he remember? What would it take to make him remember people he'd known, places he'd been? Would he ever?

Sam wished she'd never suggested a stop at the bank. Clearly Max's spirits had drooped. While he grudgingly went to see "his shrink," to pass time, Sam headed for the Hip Hop Café.

She opened the door and scanned faces, looking for a familiar one. Except for two men sitting separately at the counter, and three women at a table, who as members of the hospital auxiliary were discussing an upcoming fund-raiser, the restaurant was empty.

Because Janie socialized when she had free time, after she delivered Sam's iced tea, Sam thought she would return. Looking up from pouring sugar in her drink, she saw Janie at the counter talking to a pretty, fresh-faced young woman.

Slender with shoulder-length, sun-streaked, light-brown hair, the woman fixed a stare on the three children standing outside the café.

One of the youngsters, a girl around ten, had a firm grip on a hand of each boy. Sam guessed they were around two and five. Clearly the children were waiting for this woman who hardly looked old enough to be a mother.

"Heather, I can't believe my eyes," Janie was saying. "You're back."

Tiredness traveled from Heather's weak smile to soft brown eyes. "I don't know if you heard that my father passed away."

"No, I didn't." Janie was quick to add, "I'm sorry."

"Thank you." Heather's gaze shifted to her children once more. Anyone could see she was a devoted mother.

Sam felt a pang in the vicinity of her heart. She'd never planned on a family. Her mother's poor record at marriage hardly boded well for Sam's success at connubial bliss. And an adage came to mind: like mother, like daughter. That was how she used to think. Now she wanted all that her mother had searched for. She longed for a family of her own, a family with Max.

At the scrape of chair legs, Sam lifted her head and saw Janie rounding the counter away from the woman she'd called Heather.

"I inherited my father's ranch," Heather was saying. "And I need plenty of help."

"You should be able to find that." Janie dug in a drawer behind the counter and handed Heather three suckers for her kids.

"Thanks." Heather sent another sidelong glance in her kids' direction.

"What kind of help do you need?" Janie asked while returning to Heather's side.

"The ranch will need a lot of fixing up before I can sell it." Heather spoke with an exuberance that sounded strained. "I need to find a good, cheap handyman. Could I post this sign for one on your bulletin board?"

"Oh, sure," Janie ushered her to the board where locals had tacked notices of car and boat sales, of part-time jobs, of church and local events. "And I'll keep an eye out for someone to help."

"I'd appreciate that." Heather pushed a tack into her notice. "I'd better go. The kids get impatient quickly."

"They're all so cute."

Heather's smile stretched with parental pride. "Thank you."

As she hurried outside, Janie returned to Sam with a frosty-looking pitcher of iced tea.

"I heard you call her Heather," Sam said.

Janie filled Sam's glass before answering, "Heather Johnson. She used to live here. I thought she'd never be back after she left her daddy's ranch. People change. Don't know if she plans to stay around." Janie swiveled a look toward the window. Outside, Heather was crouched and opening the sucker wrappers. "Isn't she the sweetest-looking thing? And can you imagine having a figure like that after three kids?"

"I'm impressed," Sam said between sips on her straw.

"She looks just like her mother," Janie said about Heather.

When Sam had been fifteen, she and her mother had dressed alike. People had thought her mother was her sister. That was something Teresa Carter had strived for.

"But Heather is nothing like her mother was. Different personalities," Janie simply said.

In some ways, Sam and her mother had been opposites, too. Teresa, renamed Tyne by herself, loved partying, going out. Sam had longed for a family life. Carl Hansen would always be a fond memory as the one stepdad who'd given that to Sam for a while. But Teresa had been bored with him. She'd always grown restless, wanting to go somewhere new, find someone else. Sam had never understood why her mother had never been satisfied with her life.

For a long moment she stared with unseeing eyes at the amber-colored liquid in her glass. She and her mother really weren't alike, she mused.

Her own thought astonished her. Maybe because they'd looked so much alike, because people had always mentioned their "sunshiny smiles," their bubbly personalities, Sam had made that assumption. True, they both had liked meeting people, had been exuberant about doing new things, but the similarities had ended there. Unlike Teresa who'd leaned on a man, who'd needed one, Sam had been independent, lived a lot of years without a man in her life.

Sam set down her spoon. All these years she'd believed happiness would elude her because her mother had never found it. But her mother hadn't wanted what she did. And just because her mother couldn't make a relationship last didn't mean she couldn't, Sam realized. Unlike her, Sam knew that she didn't need to keep looking somewhere else for her happiness. She knew she'd find it with Max.

With the ring of the bell above the door, she brought herself back to her surroundings and heard Janie's good-natured groan. "Time for the third degree," she quipped.

Sam watched as Lily Mae Wheeler ambled in and took her usual seat in the first booth. The town's busybody called the Hip Hop her second home. "Was that Heather Johnson I saw?" Lily Mae asked while shifting on the booth seat to ensure she'd be at the right angle to see the door, the register and the restaurant.

"Sure was," Janie confirmed.

"What is she doing back here? You did find out, didn't you? Is she divorced? That's what I'd heard." Her voice trailed off and her attention shifted, distracted by Max's coming in.

"That didn't take long," Sam said with his approach.

"I fired him." Max took a seat across from her.

Sam refrained from responding to his comment about his psychiatrist as Janie came over.

"Can I get you something?"

"No, but thanks," he answered.

"Thanks?" She sounded shocked he'd said it. "Okay. If either of you wants anything, let me know."

Discomfort lingered in Max's eyes. He shook his head in the manner of disbelief. "If asked, friends would probably warn you to stay clear of me."

Jessica had subtly done just that. "Why would they? Max Montgomery is considered the most eligible bachelor in town. Rich. A little handsome." She teased him and rocked her hand in a "maybe" gesture. Actually he was gorgeous.

She saw him grin as she'd hoped. "What else?" he prodded.

"Intelligent," she admitted. Loving.

"We've caught someone's eagle eye," Max said, looking past her.

Turning, Sam noticed Lily Mae was practically twisting her neck out of joint to watch them. "That's Lily Mae, the town crier." She paused, waiting until he met her stare again. "Max, why aren't you going back to the doctor?"

"The shrink," he corrected.

She heard an edge to his voice.

"He can't help me remember. And if I had to hear him say one more time, 'Tell me what you think,' I'd have slugged him."

Sam knew he was only half joking. Lately she'd

sensed his patience was being stretched to its limit. Every morning, he awakened before her as if growing restless at not remembering. And he'd go to bed with her, but had trouble falling asleep. She'd wonder if anger at not remembering kept him awake. "I know it's difficult not to be discouraged."

"Hell, I thought I'd be rid of this," he said pointedly, touching the cast on his arm. When they'd been in the doctor's office, he'd been annoyed that the doctor hadn't removed the cast.

Max watched concern etch a line between her brows and gave himself a mental kick for acting like a jerk. What was the point of the self-pity, especially when it made her fret? "Forget it," he said. "I expected more than I should have."

"No, you have every right to expect to be healed by now. Having patience is the hardest part of recovering. But you will get rid of that soon."

If someone else had said that to him, he'd have half listened. But it was the sincerity in Sam's voice that made him believe her. Sometimes she seemed so serious, so different from the woman who wore a neon-green baseball cap when she jogged at dawn, or who burst into laughter when he flicked television channels and she caught a minute Bugs Bunny segment. It seemed as if he was always learning something new about her.

When they'd first met, he'd thought her flighty, didn't understand her, couldn't imagine having a thing in common. From his life-style and what he'd learned about himself, he assumed that he preferred elegant-looking women, bluebloods who'd come from a similar background. He wasn't sure he would like that man, the one who might be too blind by his social position, too ambitious, too distant to appreciate her. Standing, he picked up the bill Janie had dropped on the table earlier. "Let's go."

Sam kept a close eye on him for a long moment. The dark mood seemed to have passed, at least for now. But there would be more. He was one of the walking wounded with a huge, hidden sore.

Leading the way to the door, Sam knew that to ignore Lily Mae would result in more gossip. "'Bye, Lily Mae," she said in passing.

"Goodbye, Samantha." Speculation oozed from her voice.

Sam waited at the door until Max paid the bill. "That woman makes a career of finding out others' business," she murmured low. "She'll gossip about us."

When they'd stepped outside, Max bent his head and kissed her. It was a quick kiss, yet long enough to catch Lily Mae's attention.

Sam stayed near a second longer. "Not a wise thing to do."

Max wondered how to make her understand. He'd believed his life would be empty until he found himself. He knew now that didn't matter. It would only be empty if he lived it without her. "I don't care about her or anyone. Only you." He fit her against him. "Hell of a place to tell you this," he admitted. *I love you.* He thought the words. He felt the emotion, but the words wouldn't come out. Why not? He did love her, so why couldn't he say the words? "I don't want this to end, Sam," he said instead.

Stunned, Sam stared at him, her heart thudding harder. She'd yearned for him to say something like that, but never believed he would. Now that he had, she felt all good sense threatening to flee. *Oh, Mama, why of all the things did I inherit your romantic heart?* "Max, when I'm done working for—"

"I'm not talking about the job, Sam. I'm talking about us."

Us. Sam wanted to believe. She didn't want to listen to the little voice nagging at her. *After he has his memory back, will he believe you don't belong in his world?*

"I'm no poet, Sam." He laughed self-deprecatingly. "But I know what I feel about you." Gently he fingered a strand of her hair. "You take my breath away."

And he stopped her heart. His hadn't been words to persuade her to do something, or to coax her into his bed. They were simple words said beneath the brightness of day on the sidewalk outside the Hip Hop. Words that overwhelmed her. No one had ever said something so wonderful to her before. But, oh, God, one of them had to be sensible, didn't they? Oh, why did she? She loved him. What else mattered? With her fingertips, she stroked his cheek, steadied herself with a deep breath. She knew she wasn't her mother. Unlike her, she could have love, make it last. Closing the inches between them, she wanted to say everything that was in her heart. She was a word away from revealing all of her fears about them, telling him that she loved him.

The moment eluded them.

"Sheriff's bringing him in," a man across the street yelled from the curb to anyone who would listen.

With Max, Sam rounded a look toward the police station.

"What the hell is happening?" Max murmured.

Twelve

Sam traced his stare to the sheriff's car braking at the curb in front of the station. Before she and Max crossed the street, a crowd had congregated. Voices buzzed as Deputy Sloan Ravencrest slid out of the cruiser and cast the gawking onlookers a scowl. Like them, Sam wondered who was in the back seat, who'd been arrested. Moving to stand behind Sheriff Rafe Rawlings, Sloan opened the back door and urged a man from the car.

A tall, lean Native American, his hands cuffed behind his back, stood and was sandwiched between the sheriff and Sloan. "Oh, my gosh," Sam muttered as the man was swiftly ushered toward the door of the police station. The gossipmongers at the hospital would have a field day. Back straight, head up, Gavin

Nighthawk was still wearing his hospital lab coat. They'd apparently arrested him while the highly respected doctor had been at work at Whitehorn Memorial. "What's happening?" she asked a woman beside her, the owner of a neighboring dress shop.

Instead of answering, the woman looked from Sam to Max. "Hello, Mr. Montgomery."

Clearly, by the questions in Max's eyes, he had no idea who she was, but he nodded hello.

"I heard Gavin Nighthawk was arrested for Christina Montgomery's—for your sister's murder," she said to Max.

Sam dared a look at him. The only outward change in his appearance came from a slight narrowing of his eyes.

Max said nothing, waiting until they'd distanced themselves from the woman and the crowd. Without another word, he pivoted toward the sheriff's office.

One of the deputies signaled their approach because Rafe Rawlings whipped around when they were feet away. "Mr. Montgomery."

At the railing, Max paused, Sam with him. "What's happening here, Sheriff?"

"Sloan, take him in," Rafe said to his deputy about their prisoner.

While Sloan hurried Gavin into the building, the sheriff came up to Max and Sam to keep their conversation private.

"Someone said you arrested him for Christina's murder," Max prodded. "Did he confess? Does Ellis know?"

"We haven't notified him yet." Rafe spoke low. "Nighthawk contends he's innocent. We're arresting him on various evidence."

"What kind of evidence?"

"DNA. It proved that Gavin Nighthawk is the father of the baby your sister had. We figure he might have wanted your sister to keep that quiet. His career is important to him," he added, seeming to view that as a motive for killing her. "I imagine your father will be relieved to have this over." Rafe cupped a hand over Max's shoulder. "It hasn't been easy for any of you."

Max gave him the expected nod of thanks, but he turned a frown on Sam when they were alone. "I'm not a part of this," he said while they were walking toward her vehicle.

As if nothing unusual had happened, neither of them said more about Gavin Nighthawk. Unlike what Max believed, Sam felt that Max couldn't disassociate himself. If he didn't have the amnesia, he would want someone accountable for his sister's murder. That was a normal reaction to the death of a loved one. In time, if more memories returned, he'd know that.

By the time they reached the house, heavy gray clouds had gathered. As Sam expected, several phone messages needed Max's attention. One was from his father. While he returned the calls, Sam wandered upstairs to her room to change her clothes.

With not much time before dinner, she showered quickly. Wrapping a towel around her, she blow-dried her hair, then wandered to the closet. The day had been a difficult one for Max. So many images, so many happenings.

By nature, she was a talker. If something or someone bothered her, she never reined in her feelings.

Max was the opposite. A brooder, he would mull over something, gnaw at it.

Sam wiggled into a new green print slip dress, then bent to retrieve her fancy sandals from the back of the closet. She wished he would share what he was feeling with her, let her help. Even if she couldn't heal his troubled thoughts, she could comfort. Her hair slightly damp, she fluffed the strands with her fingers as she started down the stairs.

Though Josie served them breakfast in the kitchen as Max had requested, she refused to serve dinner anywhere except in the formal dining room. She'd set a perfect table with candles in silver candlesticks, fine crystal and china.

Sam had entered the room only seconds before Max.

As his eyes swept appreciatively over her, she nearly blushed.

"You look lovely."

She'd wanted just such a response from him, but feeling a little self-conscious, she laughed. "Thank you." She had spiffed up more than usual tonight. She'd felt different, more feminine after his earlier words to her. She thought back to those moments when he'd told her he didn't want this to end. She wanted to believe that was possible. She wanted to let herself feel loved.

And wise or not, she wanted desperately to let herself believe this was a beginning for them.

Her heart filled with love, she soaked in the sight of him as he looked down to pour the white wine into a fluted glass for her. The slightest of frown lines marred his brow. Later, when his mind wasn't troubled, she would tell him what she felt. She would tell him that she loved him.

Now she had another matter to deal with. Sam took a seat at the table. When he joined her and handed her the wineglass, his lips widened to a smile. But it failed to reach his eyes. Sam made a logical assumption. "Max, do you want to talk about what happened in town?"

"I guess the real Max Montgomery is emerging," he mocked. "Everyone has said I was cold and indifferent. That's how I feel about Christina. I really don't feel anything."

Sam reached for his hand, so near hers on the table, and linked her fingers with his. "You can't make yourself feel something."

"I don't remember her, Sam. She's a name to me, nothing more. Should I be angry at Gavin Nighthawk? Should I be relieved Christina's alleged killer has been caught? I don't know what to feel."

She heard the depth of frustration in him.

"Who knows?" He pulled her hand to him and kissed her palm. "The truth is that neither of us knows what I'm really like. What I'll be like when I can remember again."

Sam searched his face. "What makes you think you'll change?"

"According to other people, I'm not like I was before the accident," he pointed out. "Logic dictates that when my memory returns I'll revert to the way I was."

She'd known a softer, gentler version of Max Montgomery—but not for a moment did she fool herself. The workaholic, practical and no-nonsense man existed. "Had your father heard about the arrest?" she asked, remembering how agitated Ellis had sounded when Max played his message on the answering machine.

"He did." Max released her hand and reached for his wineglass. "He's ranting about a quick trial, about bringing the monster to justice."

"What did you say?"

"What could I say? Did Nighthawk do it?" Max sipped his wine. "Do you think so?"

Sam would have been guessing. "I don't know. I do know there's been a lot of pressure on the sheriff to find the killer."

"From my father?"

"Oh, yes."

"He throws his weight around, doesn't he?"

Remaining silent, she responded with a slim smile.

Puzzlement swept across his face. "Did I?"

She knew the answer to that. The Montgomerys, especially Ellis, had expected preferential treatment. Rachel seemed more down-to-earth to Sam, but then she'd been away for a while, away from her father's influence.

And Max? What had he been like? She didn't think

he'd bend easily to someone else's way, but most of his life, he'd seemed to have done what his father had expected of him. According to other people, Max Montgomery had been just as ambitious, just as demanding, as his father. Sam refrained from pointing that out to Max. He had enough doubts about himself because of the amnesia.

After a dinner of poached salmon and hazelnut cake for dessert, Sam cajoled Max into a game of chess for a penny a point. She won, more the result of his lack of concentration than her skill.

With time to spare before Alyssa arrived, Sam wandered out to the terrace. She thought Max might want to be alone, but only a few minutes passed and he joined her. As he slid an arm across her stomach and pressed her back against him, she smiled, glad he'd come outside. With evening, more clouds filled the sky, blocking the light of the moon. The scent of incoming rain floated on the breeze. Resting her head back on his shoulder, she watched the shadow of a prairie dog scoot into tall grass. "You should get horses."

"A dog. Horses." A trace of amusement edged his voice. "What's next? An elephant?"

Sam cracked a small grin at his teasing.

"Do you ride?" he asked.

"Yes. I learned when we were living in Texas."

Lightly he pressed his lips to her hair. "I'll think about it, then."

Sam angled a smile back at him. Warm with love for him, she needed no coaxing. She turned in his embrace.

"Through something bad, I've found something wonderful." He kissed the tip of her nose. "You."

Desperately Sam wanted to believe in them. Was this—hope—what her mother had felt all those times? Sam understood now. Not desire, but hope in a future with someone had led her mother.

Like a butterfly's caress, his mouth grazed hers. The kiss was sweet, inviting. "Hmm," she murmured. "Is there time?" She sighed as his fingers played across her hip. No answer was needed. She closed her eyes, drifting beneath the caress of his hand down her thigh, as one kiss blended into another.

Barely, they got dressed in time. Sam was slipping on her dress when the doorbell rang. While Max hurried down the stairs, she wiggled her feet into her sandals, then rushed out of the bedroom. Though all day she'd looked forward to spending time with Alyssa, she wished now that she and Max would be alone tonight.

When Sam reached the top of the staircase, she heard Rachel's hello to her brother.

Sam hit the bottom step to see Rachel halting in midstride and placing a hand on her stomach. "Oh, boy. Oh, girl."

Despite the laughter in her eyes, a concerned Max rushed to her. "Are you okay?"

Behind Rachel, standing in the doorway, Jack chuckled. "This baby is a live wire."

"Feel," Rachel urged Max.

He hesitated. "No, that's okay."

"Come on, Max." Rachel took his hand and placed it on her stomach. "Feel."

Immediately a light came into his eyes. "Damn," he whispered. "I feel it. It's moving all over the place."

"That's nothing," Rachel assured him. "Sometimes, like late at night," she said, looking over her shoulder at Jack for confirmation, "I think the baby is rocking in there."

"It's the truth," Jack said with a proud father-to-be grin. Moving into the living room, he lowered a sleeping Alyssa to the sofa.

"She'll be awake in a few minutes," Rachel told Max. "After an hour with her, you're probably going to wish you weren't so eager for this playtime." Rachel set down the diaper bag. "There's one filled bottle in the bag, Sam. Sometimes Alyssa still looks for it."

Sam smiled with her. She expected no problem. She'd gotten to know Alyssa during one of Rachel's visits at the hospital.

In the silent way of a married couple, Rachel exchanged a look with Jack.

"Is there something you want to say?" Max questioned.

Rachel tipped her head slightly in a quizzical manner. "Did you hear about Gavin?"

"We were there when Sheriff Rawlings and Sloan were bringing him in," Sam answered.

"We know now that the father's note left with Alyssa was from Gavin," Jack said.

Max regarded Alyssa. "If evidence proves he's the murderer, chances are you'll be keeping Alyssa."

"You know how I feel about Alyssa," Rachel said, "but I don't hope for her father to have killed her mother. That's not something I'd want her to have to grow up knowing."

"Well, was there any other special man?"

Jack moved near Rachel and touched the small of her back as if offering moral support.

"I don't recall her mentioning anyone else. I know that for a while Gavin was with Patricia Winthrop," Rachel informed them.

Max faced Sam, as if looking to her for an explanation. She knew he had no idea who the woman was. "She's extremely beautiful with her white-blond hair," she said, thinking he might have noticed her when they were in town. "She's a member of the country club set."

"And she was seeing Gavin Nighthawk?"

"They weren't a match her family would dream of. Eventually she spurned him and who knows who was next in his life."

Jack shifted his stance. "Rachel, we should leave or—"

"We'll be late," she finished for him and smiled before she went to Alyssa to kiss her cheek. Lacing her fingers with Jack's, she wandered with him toward the door.

Sam glanced at a window and observed Ellis's car pulling in the driveway. "Your father just arrived."

"He's acting strange," Rachel said to Max. "He's

been…oddly attentive. I think he's grooming himself to be a grandpa."

Humor rose in Max. "Now, there's a thought. He'll probably take the kid on the campaign trail to show his family man traits."

The sounds of the puppy's yipping drew Sam to the kitchen. "Have fun," she called to Rachel and Jack, and left to get the pup. But when within seconds she returned with it, she heard Rachel's laugh and gathered she and Jack had gotten stalled at the front door by Ellis.

"Max and Sam are baby-sitting," Rachel was explaining. With Jack, she inched closer to the doorway. "Wait until you see Max's puppy," she said to her father. "He's so cute."

"His what?"

With that, Rachel and Jack made their escape.

Ellis glanced to his left toward Sam and the puppy. "What possessed you to get a dog? Who's going to care for him?" A scowl replaced his frown. "You don't have time, Max."

No, he had no time for anything but his work, did he? Max mused. Was that the kind of thinking that had driven him for years? Had he been happy? Successful, yes. But happy?

On the floor now, the pup nudged the ball around the highly polished wood in the den. He slapped a paw at the ball, sent it rolling across the room and scampered after it, skidding on all fours. He came to a stop and plopped on the area rug with its Native American design, as if suddenly bored with playing.

"Are you going to keep it?" Ellis questioned.

Max felt Sam's glance. "I don't know," he answered, but he knew he would. Sam would be heartbroken if he got rid of the dog. As if sensing acceptance, the puppy looked up at him and tapped its tail on the floor.

Critically, Ellis eyed the pup. "You always wanted one, you know. Do you remember that?"

Max shot a look at him. Age nine. He could see himself. Feel a loneliness seeping into him. He'd asked for a dog, longed for one of his own. He'd thought no one had been listening when he'd asked to have one.

Max felt his heart quicken. He'd just had a memory, a vivid one of the last time he'd talked about a pet. His mother had breezily prattled on about some charity she was chairing, as if he'd never spoken. And his father? Max recalled Ellis drinking his morning coffee, nodding in response to Max's mother. But for a brief second he had looked in Max's direction. He had been paying attention to him, he realized now.

"Your mother didn't abide by pets," Ellis said. "She thought they were too dirty. As a kid I had two dogs. A Boston terrier and a golden retriever." He motioned toward the puppy. "What kind is this?"

Sam dug into the diaper bag that Rachel had left. "A collie mix."

He'd cared, Max knew now. A hell of a thing. But at thirty-four, he'd learned that his father, in his own way, had cared about him and his feelings—always had.

Was that the first of many memories? Max wondered.

The warming glow of a setting sun filled the room and enticed him toward the terrace doors. The sky bore a rainbow of colors, streaks of pink and orange shooting across the horizon.

"So what's its name?" Ellis asked.

"What did you name yours?" Sam replied because Max had suddenly gone silent.

"The terrier was Putts and—"

"Putts?" Over his shoulder, Max chuckled.

Ellis shrugged, looking embarrassed. "And the other one was Casey."

Though no one asked for her opinion, Sam wasn't shy to give it. "Cute name."

Max exchanged a grin with her. "Name him that."

A vague smile sparkled in Ellis's eyes. "He was a fine dog. Mine, that is. This one might be, too," he said, giving the puppy another look.

Max stared out the window again and took a sharp breath as another memory flashed at him. He'd remembered Ellis talking about his parents, driving by the closed-up factory to show it to Max. "My father worked there," he'd said.

Max remembered more. His grandparents had been strict and not financially well off, but hardworking. Ellis had told him he would never have had anything if he hadn't worked hard.

Max assumed that because his father hadn't had much as a child he'd grown ambitious. He'd said that his money had come from selling the family land. He was a self-made man who'd caught the eye of a woman with a pedigree. And today, Max mused, Ellis had money, social position and power. Was that why for years Max, too, hadn't wanted anything else?

Behind him, Ellis cleared his throat in the manner of someone aware how uncharacteristic he was acting. "Why I came is because of Nighthawk. We need to talk."

Max faced him. Ellis stayed only twenty minutes, but was adamant that the prosecutor seek the death penalty. Before he stood to leave, he'd calmed a little. His eyes went to a sleeping Alyssa. "Do you know what you're doing?"

Max looked at Alyssa, and Sam, then back to his father. "We'll be fine." Not quite so confident, he waited until they were alone to question Sam's baby-sitting skills. "We will be, won't we?"

Sam stifled a laugh. "Losing your nerve?"

He eyed Alyssa again. Who wouldn't have misgivings about caring for someone so small?

"Relax." Sam sidestepped him. "You'll be fine. I have to put this in the refrigerator," she said about the bottle.

"Don't be long," Max called after her.

He heard her laugh. At him or with him? It didn't matter. When he'd been in the hospital, fighting depression over the amnesia, he'd thought he'd never smile again. She'd made the difference. She'd made him feel whole again.

At the sound of rain pattering against the window, Max peered outside, then moved closer to the baby. He really wanted contact with the little one. In what he viewed as a dumb reaction, he tensed as she suddenly stirred. A tiny foot flexed, then a chubby leg stretched.

Max inched closer. He'd seen a movie called *Raiders of the Lost Ark* recently with Sam. In one scene, the hero, an archaeologist, carefully measured each step to not set off some booby trap with the wrong move.

Max realized he felt a bit like that character as he approached Alyssa. She was an unknown to him and that bothered him. But if he couldn't feel any closeness for Christina, finding it with her baby might be the next best thing.

Less anxious, he neared the little one just as her head turned in his direction. Lashes fluttered, then her eyes opened wide to him. "Hi, sweetheart," he said softly, soothingly because she looked ready to burst into tears.

Sam, come back now. Max glanced at the doorway. How long did it take to place a bottle of milk in the refrigerator? If she was deliberately deserting him, he'd—

He saw Alyssa's brows furrow. "Want to come here?" Max held out an arm to her. *Just don't cry. Don't cry.*

A second passed. Then another. He felt as if he were being scrutinized by one of the best before she started moving toward him. Max took it as a sign of approval and bent to lift her against him.

"Ba-ba."

What did that mean? "I don't know what you want. Wait until the resident expert returns. Okay?"

"Ba-ba."

Max laughed. Definitely she had a limited vocabulary. "Okay, gotcha. Ba-ba. What's that mean? Bottle?" His voice trailed off.

A smile, so bright it warmed his insides, spread across her face. She was so beautiful. He stared into blue eyes, sparkling blue eyes that would one day capture a man's soul. Incredible blue eyes. Blue eyes just like Christina's.

Oh, God. Christina. His gut clenched. "Christina." The word came out choked. Unexpected grief swept through him, clutched his heart. It could have been yesterday. Vividly he remembered that moment when he'd learned she was dead.

Dead. A breath hitched in his throat. Eyes squeezed tight, he pulled Alyssa to him, cuddled his sister's baby, held her tightly. Too tightly, he feared, feeling her squirm. Because he was afraid to hold her, he set her down on the carpet. It took effort to think, to focus on anything, but he saw the toys, a fabric book, a ball that jingled. Max placed them in front of her, then sank to a sofa cushion. Fast and furious, images bombarded him. And one haunted him.

He saw himself in his office, the phone in his hand. "I need you," his sister was saying. "Max, everything is going wrong. I don't know who else to call."

Tears broke her voice. He'd heard them and steeled himself against the softness flowing through him, making him want to help her.

But why? Why hadn't he helped her? Why hadn't

he met his sister? "I'm busy. Too busy," he remembered saying. Too busy for what?

Why? Why had he refused her? If only he hadn't, if only—what? Nothing would be different. Christina would still be gone, but she'd know, wouldn't she? She'd know that he'd loved her.

Guilt swept over him, squeezed at his throat. He shut his eyes again, felt the sting of tears behind his lids while more images of his past flashed by. He couldn't help her—or anyone. That's why he hadn't met her. He'd learned years ago that he hurt people. Look at what he'd done to Michelle.

Oh, God.

He'd nearly killed a woman.

All he'd forgotten descended on him. Michelle had been the first one he'd hurt. Rachel hadn't told him everything. It had been during finals week at college. He'd been studying all night. He'd been tired. Exhausted. He should have never gotten behind the steering wheel. The accident had been his fault. A woman had suffered months in the hospital, months of agony in rehabilitation because of him, because of his arrogance.

Her only mistake had been loving him. People who loved him got hurt. That's what he hadn't remembered. That's what he wanted to forget. Pictures raced through his mind. If only he could stop thinking, feeling.

Thirteen

It was the look on his face that stalled Sam in the doorway. He looked pale, as if all the blood had drained from his face. She checked on Alyssa. Happily she patted the jingling ball. Sam still didn't move. She couldn't. He kept staring at the photograph of Christina. What was happening here? In the darkening room, Sam stepped forward slowly, quietly.

A few feet from him, she saw his face in profile, saw the tears on his cheek. He'd remembered. Sam didn't need confirmation from him. Anguish deepened the lines bracketing his mouth. He sat like a battered man, as if even breathing was too much work.

Oh, Max. Her breath stuck in her throat at seeing so much pain in his face. She remained silent, even as she sat beside him. Outside rain fell, plopping in a syncopated beat against the roof of the house. She listened to it, still said nothing, and waited.

Minutes passed. She had no idea how much time passed before he became aware of her and finally spoke. "I remember it all. Christina's call, the break in her voice." He shut his eyes as if what he could see was too painful. "She was on the verge of tears when she asked me to meet her. I refused. It was the last time I talked to her." His voice softened in the manner of someone struggling to talk. "I knew something was wrong, something was troubling her, but I was busy at the bank, and didn't take the time to help her. Then no one knew where she was."

Quiet, he simply stared at the photograph. Before he spoke again, he labored for a breath. "I nearly went crazy when we couldn't find her. Rachel came. That helped. But our father was ranting about Christina's irresponsibleness, as if she was taking up too much of his time."

Sam remembered feeling terrible for the family. Every day in the newspaper an article appeared, rehashing Christina's disappearance and who her family was.

"There was no comfort when we learned where she was, what happened to her. She was dead. She'd never be back. Never," he said so softly that the word was lost on the air.

Sam fought against tears for him. All that had been hidden within him was visible now.

"I offered a huge reward for information leading to

the arrest of the person responsible. So what? I couldn't make up for what I hadn't done. That phone call had been her cry for help."

"Max, there were others she could have called."

His gaze strayed to her. "No, there wasn't. You don't understand. Rachel wasn't in town back then. And our father was always busy. Even when Christina was younger, mourning our mother's death, he was never there for her. Sure, she was wild. She was trying to get his attention. That's why she went from man to man. And I wasn't any better than him. She expected me to be there for her, and I wasn't."

Max bowed his head. He wanted to backtrack to the day Christina had phoned him, to run from the bank and meet her. He wanted to tell her he was sorry. He wanted her back.

"Damn it," he murmured, and jerked, startled when Sam touched his forearm. Stay clear of me, he should say to her. As if it was yesterday, he could see Michelle inside the dark confines of the car. Limp, she sat in the passenger's seat, her head back, blood from a gash on her forehead streaking her cheek. Her moan filled his mind. Mercifully he saw the sudden flashing red light of an ambulance.

"Help me," she'd cried.

How could he? He didn't know how to help—only hurt.

He'd hurt her, hurt Christina.

That one thought hammered in his head. Who next? he wondered, and looked at Sam. He couldn't be near her, near her sweetness; he didn't deserve her gentleness. Peripherally he saw her lean closer. Before she made contact, he rushed to his feet, stepped away, using the desk as a barrier between them.

"Max?"

He heard bewilderment in her voice, but kept walking out the terrace doors and into the rain. He needed to be alone, to think about the past and about the future that he wouldn't—couldn't—have with her now.

He needed to do right by her. A flash of lightning illuminated surrounding trees. Max walked slowly, letting the rain pour over him. Two women had already suffered at his hands. Why? Why had he let himself get this close to Sam?

He swore under his breath. He hadn't been thinking straight. He'd made the biggest mistake of his life while he'd had the amnesia. He'd fallen in love with her. He'd begun to believe in a future with her. He never would have let it go this far if he hadn't had amnesia, hadn't been so addled. With his memory came the truth of who he really was. He hurt people. He was no good for Sam. As long as he kept his distance, she would be safe.

With an ache lumping in his throat, he strode back to the terrace doors, stepped into the room. Sitting on the carpet with Alyssa, Sam cast a look of uncertainty at him. He couldn't weaken. He had to make the break now. *I'm sorry, Sam.* She'd never know how sorry he was.

"Max, let me help."

He never doubted she would want to. She possessed a generous heart. Giving came so naturally to her.

As she stood and started to reach out to him, he fought himself. "Don't." He couldn't be gentler. He might fold, might let her see how desperate he was to have her in his arms. Even as hurt flashed in her eyes, he told himself that he was doing right by her. He was saving her from more heartache, much more. "Everything is different now."

"Different?" Her head moved slightly in a little shake as if she were trying to clear muddled thoughts.

She wasn't dumb; she was confused, he realized. Why wouldn't she be? One moment he caressed her like a captivated lover, and the next he shunned her touch. But he couldn't afford to give in to the love consuming him. This beautiful woman with her sunshine smile and quick wit who gentled him with a touch and challenged him with her sharp tongue meant everything to him. And he'd die before he'd hurt her, too.

"What do you mean?" Sam watched a stream of water cut across his jaw and down his neck. "Different?"

"I have my memory back. I don't need a nurse."

A nurse? Or me? Sam breathed slowly and deeply. Needing contact with someone was overwhelming her. Nearby on the carpet, Alyssa batted at the ball and babbled. Sam pivoted toward her, gathered her in her arms.

"You can go, Sam."

Just like that. How calmly he'd said the words when she could hardly speak, breathe. She'd played mind games with herself, she acknowledged. She'd told herself that when he got his memory back, everything would be different. But she'd never believed this would really happen, never prepared for the hurt. "Go?"

"We don't belong together," he said simply.

And she wanted to weep.

Weren't those the words she'd expected and had never wanted to hear? Foolish. She was so foolish. She'd known he wouldn't want her once he remembered who he was. She'd known they'd never be together forever. She couldn't argue, couldn't find any words to stop what was happening. She'd always known all she'd found with him was bound to end.

"You need to go."

She looked for a hint of emotion in his eyes, some indication that he didn't mean what he was saying. She saw nothing. There was a meanness about him suddenly. People were right. He could hurt someone who cared about him, could hurt them and not look back. With more effort than she imagined she would need, she mouthed necessary words. "I'll inform Rachel that she should hire a new physical therapist."

"Do that."

Pressure building in her chest, she wanted to run out of the room. But Samantha Lynn Carter was made of sturdier stock. She'd never been a weepy female and didn't plan to start now. With Alyssa in her arms, she left the room and climbed the stairs.

Almost instantly when Sam set Alyssa down on the bedroom carpet, she whined. To distract her, Sam placed a jingling ball on the floor in front of her. Once her small hand touched it, she forgot she wasn't being held.

Anger mingling with her hurt, Sam searched for anything to stay busy. At home, she'd have scrubbed floors. Here, she chose the most logical act.

She went to the closet and yanked a suitcase from the shelf. Leaving in the middle of the evening had never been part of her plan. Because she never forgot responsibilities, she would, of course, stay until Rachel returned for the little one. But not a moment longer.

Her throat tightening, threatening to choke her, she slammed the suitcase onto the bed. Then she sank to the mattress and she gave in to the smarting tears. Why had she given him her heart? *Oh, Sam, you're such an idiot. He never loved you. He never said those words.* That was what she'd forgotten to remember. She'd had her own form of amnesia, not allowing herself to face facts. He'd only felt dependent on her while he'd had amnesia. She'd fooled herself into believing that what she wanted most in life was within reach. It wasn't. Never would be. All that they'd shared had been about his need for her.

Straightening, she brushed the back of her hand at wet tears. Enough. Tears wouldn't change anything. In a rush of movement, she stuffed clothes in the suitcase. She should have known this day would come. Fool. She was such a fool. Her mother's foolish child. And an even more foolish woman had believed that Max Montgomery would want forever with her.

For most of the evening she stayed closeted in her room with Alyssa. She never bothered to find out where Max was. She cared for Alyssa, played with her, fed her dinner and changed her diaper, then held her until she fell asleep again.

At ten o'clock, expecting Rachel and Jack at any moment, she carried a sleeping Alyssa downstairs.

"We're back," a voice called from the foyer as Sam descended the staircase.

With Rachel's return, Sam mentally geared up for the next difficult moments. Carrying Alyssa in her arms, she ambled toward the sound of voices and into the living room.

Max had already appeared. Not looking Sam's way, he made small talk with his sister. "Samantha handled the baby-sitting duties," he told Rachel. Before Rachel asked, he made an excuse for not spending time with Alyssa. "I was tired, so she took over."

"Are you all right?"

A mirthless smile curved his lips. "Just tired, Rachel. Nothing more."

Sam noticed he didn't tell her that his memory had returned. He ushered his sister and Jack to the door and said he'd baby-sit again sometime.

Aware of Rachel's watchful stare, Sam managed smiles at all the right moments. If Rachel detected tension between them, she said nothing. Sam waited only until Rachel and Jack pulled way, then she returned to her room.

Before Max got up in the morning, she would be gone.

It was the quietness in the house that awakened him. The rooms were the same, a morning sun still flooded the kitchen with light, but the house was empty, void of life. No radio blared from the kitchen, no soft feminine voice hummed along.

Max eased from the bed, hating the way he felt, hating the way he'd ended everything. There had been no other way. It had been best for Sam.

In retrospect, he'd say that he'd acted peculiar during his episode as an amnesiac. He'd been soft, too soft. He needed to toughen up again.

He tried to do just that.

During the next few days he fell into an old routine. At eight, as he'd done before his accident, he was already sitting at his desk in the bank. Trying to focus on something, anything, he stared at a pay increase recommendation for employees, a document that required only his signature. He held the pen point on the paper, but didn't sign it.

The words blurred. His mind's eye saw Sam instead. Every day had been the same. She wouldn't leave him alone. This morning he remembered the way she'd looked basking by the pool, her skin golden and glowing; the slight curve of her lips when they'd parted for his kiss; the golden threads glistening among the red strands of her hair when she'd stood in the sunlight. She was like a haunting apparition, appearing everywhere, as if determined to make him suffer, to drive him crazy.

Unable to concentrate, he pushed away from his desk. He was miserable now without her. And his only solace came from knowing that she was better off without him. While he'd had the amnesia, he'd nearly forgotten what was really important. He didn't have any business getting close to anyone ever again. If he kept his distance, then no one would get hurt.

The sound of his office door opening made him look up.

Jack grinned wryly. "Your sister sent me."

"Tell her I'm fine. I'm back to normal."

"That's what I said about you." He ambled in, closing the door behind him. "She said that's why she's worried."

Max took the gibe good-naturedly. "What's happening with the Kincaids?" he asked. With his memory back, he recalled that it was Jack and his sister Gina who'd been hired to locate Garrett's seven grandsons. Six of them had been found.

Jack retraced his steps to Max's desk. "Since we've had no luck locating Garrett Kincaid's seventh grandson here, Gina is extending her investigation to towns outside of Whitehorn."

"She thinks he's near?"

Jack nodded. "Gina's pretty intuitive. She thinks he's right under her nose."

"Last time I talked to Garrett he was determined to meet all of his grandsons."

"He's a fair man," Jack offered. "He wants to do right by them."

But Max wasn't that kind of man, was he? How close was he to being again the man disliked by so many? Looking down, he scribbled his signature on the paper for the pay raise.

"I heard he's a real bear again," a blond clerk, sitting behind the desk in the rehab center said to the nurse standing nearby.

"Mr. Scrooge, you mean." The brunette sighed. "Too bad. He's gorgeous. But I don't like brooding men. Someone else can have Max Montgomery."

Sam had no intention of eavesdropping. But Max's name being said by anyone put her on alert.

Sam felt sadness for him sweep through her. Just a week ago her world had been different, her world had included Max. Now she sat in the small break room at the rehab center, drinking coffee and lurking around to catch any news about him.

After tucking the paperback she'd bought yesterday into her shoulder bag, she drained the coffee in her cup. It seemed strange to get up for a regular job, but she'd heard from a friend that the hospital needed another physical therapist while one of the staff took her vacation. So three days ago Sam had settled into the routine.

Now at two in the afternoon, fatigue hit. She rode

the elevator to the fourth floor therapy room. Not even a jolt of caffeine had helped. Blame it on a bad night's sleep. She'd been awake for hours, thinking about Max. She wasn't pleased with herself. Enjoy. Have Fun. Don't Expect Too Much had always been her motto. Once she'd met Max, she'd forgotten that.

The swoosh of the elevator doors opening snapped her back to her surroundings. She left the elevator, determined to stop feeling sorry for herself, and entered the gymnasium-size therapy room.

A woman with a prosthesis was learning to walk with the aid of the double-bar rail. A man who was a day away from being discharged rolled his wheelchair toward the weighted pulleys. Sam strolled toward the spa to help another patient.

Hours later, when she finally had time to herself, she sat at the scarred oak desk at the back of the room.

Her supervisor, a therapist whom Sam had known since nursing school, plopped onto a chair near Sam. "Since you worked for Max Montgomery, I thought you'd want to know that the family needs a private nurse again."

"What?" Sam's heart jumped. "Who? Max?"

Jana leaned on the edge of the desk. "Rachel Henderson has been ordered to stay in bed for a few weeks."

Worry sprang forth. "Is the baby all right?"

"From what I heard, the baby is fine. And Rachel is in good spirits, according to her obstetrician. But she needs a live-in nurse. Would you—"

"Of course," Sam cut in, not waiting for her to finish

asking. "But what about here? Will I be leaving you shorthanded?"

"I called the registry. They've found another therapist for me. Go."

"Jack told me you were coming," Rachel said brightly when Sam strolled into the bedroom later that afternoon. "I'm so glad."

Sam took the hand Rachel held out to her. "I wouldn't stay away once I'd heard. We have to take care of you and your baby, don't we?" Swiftly she assessed Rachel. Her face had a rosy glow, her smile appeared genuine and free of discomfort.

"I'll be fine. The doctor worries easily." Despite her lighthearted tone, Rachel couldn't veil the trace of alarm in her eyes.

"Follow his orders and everything will be all right," Sam assured her.

"I will. Sit down," she said more seriously. "Tell me what happened with you and my brother."

Sam expected Rachel's distress about them, knew this woman whom she now considered a friend would want to know more.

"I don't know if you've heard, but he's become impossible again."

Sam hated the thought that his mind had returned him to the old Max. The man she'd fallen in love with had been happier, free of dark emotions.

"I think he misses you. My question is, do you miss him?"

Even though she'd expected Rachel's questions,

Sam wasn't really prepared to answer, to share her humiliation with her. "Rachel, what I feel doesn't matter."

"To me, it does. I know you love him. So why aren't you together?"

Sam uttered the thought haunting her. "Two people have to be in love, Rachel, not one."

"*Two* people are."

Sam fought the warmth of tears in her eyes. "No, he's not in love with me."

"Who says?"

"He did."

Rachel inclined her head questioningly. "'I don't love you.' He said that?"

"Not in those words exactly. 'Everything is different now.' Those were the words he'd said." *We don't belong together.* She didn't want to discuss Max anymore, not even with Rachel. "Let me get settled in, then I'll make us some tea."

"And we'll talk," Rachel insisted.

Sam pivoted away. They could talk endlessly. But nothing Rachel could say would make a difference. The simple truth was that Max didn't want her.

She took her time to carry her suitcase to her room and to learn her way around the kitchen. She made the tea and found some shortbread cookies in a tin.

Rachel hadn't forgotten her intentions. The moment Sam ambled in with the tray, Rachel began, "Samantha, what happened that night with Michelle affected him forever. He still blames himself, still believes if something goes wrong, it's his fault."

Busy pouring tea, Sam had been listening halfheartedly. Now Rachel's words garnered her attention. "What do you mean?"

"No one understood. No one knew about Michelle except me. And it breaks my heart. He always blamed himself for it, believing if he hadn't been so tired, then he would have reacted differently. Afterward, he isolated himself, Sam. He wouldn't allow himself to get close to anyone. People saw a ruthless, difficult man, but he only seemed that way. He put up this shield to keep his distance from everyone." Sadness for Max had stolen the glow from her face. "He believes he hurts people who care about him."

Sam set down the teapot and stared hard at Rachel for a long moment, certain she'd misunderstood.

"He thinks if people care about him, then he'll be responsible for—"

"Hurting them?" Sam finished for her.

"Yes."

"Rachel, that's absurd, ridiculous."

Rachel nodded. "I agree. But that's what he believes, especially after what happened with Christina."

Now Sam was totally lost. "I don't understand. What did he have to do with what happened to Christina?"

"Nothing. You can see that. So can I. But not him. He believes he let Christina down, too. After all, she'd called and he didn't go to her."

And now he felt responsible for hurting two people? Sam's heart twisted for the torment he carried. This was what the amnesia had given his mind a rest from. This was what Rachel had tried to protect him from remembering—his guilt.

Fourteen

"I heard you sent that nurse packing."

Max wondered who his father's source was. Ellis had acted as if he didn't like Sam. The odd thing was, he always asked about her. No longer staring out his office window, Max shifted the telephone receiver to his other ear and swiveled his desk chair around. "I don't need her."

"Guess so."

He'd swear Ellis had said those words with a different meaning in mind.

"The reason I called was to tell you about your sister."

Max opened the center desk drawer to retrieve a manila file folder. He was in no mood to rehash Nighthawk's arrest for Christina's murder. "What about Christina?"

"I'm not talking about Christina. I'm talking about Rachel. The two of you are stressing me," he said, sounding agitated. "She's been confined to bed for a few weeks."

Max shut the drawer. "When did you learn this?"

"Jack called this morning. He said nothing is wrong with the baby but they aren't taking chances."

Max was already standing. "I'll talk to you later. I've got to go."

"Where?"

"To see her." Max didn't bother to call Rachel first.

Over the previous weeks she tended to drop in, so he assumed he could do the same. "Dad told me you were taking it easy," he said when he entered her bedroom.

Rachel presented a smile meant to convince him that she was fine. "I doubt that's how he said it. Seriously, he's been helpful. Even got Sam for me."

"What?" He followed Rachel's stare behind him and saw Sam standing in the doorway. He should have expected to see her. If Rachel needed a private nurse, Sam would be the one. Briefly he wondered if the old man had gone soft on him and was playing matchmaker.

As if he was no more important than a pesky fly, she gave him a glance, no more. "I didn't know you had company, Rachel." She sounded all business. "I'll come back later."

"Sam—" Before Rachel's protest began, she'd left. "Oh, Max. Darn. Max, I've kept quiet before this, but now there's someone in your life who loves you." Sighing, Rachel shifted on the mattress as if looking for a comfortable position.

Alarmed at the hint of discomfort on her face, Max hurried to her. "Here, let me help." He reached behind her and plumped a pillow. "Better?"

"Yes." She managed what he viewed as a weak smile. "Max, she believes you never cared about her. Why are you doing this? You're hurting yourself, too."

What happened to him didn't matter. That's what Rachel didn't understand. She wasn't helping, wasn't making this easy on him. Everything that he wanted to forget was back with him again. He had thought he was learning to live his life without Sam. He'd been wrong, he knew now. "I don't want to hurt someone else that I love."

Rachel turned compassionate eyes up at him. "Like Sam?"

"Yes, I love her." Irritated that she'd gotten the admittance out of him, he stood to escape the look in her eyes. "But what difference does that make?" With his own words still echoing in his head, he found himself staring at Sam.

Standing in the doorway, she tilted her head slightly. How much had she heard? Puzzlement clouded her gaze. Or was that longing? Don't, he berated himself. She deserves better than you.

It took effort to remember why she'd come into the room, Sam realized. When she'd seen him, she'd wanted to give in to all her loneliness for him. Then she'd heard his words. They lingered in her mind now as she spoke to Rachel. "I'm sorry to interrupt, Rachel. But your medicine is on the table beside you. You need to take it." Sam turned and left the room before emotion snuck in on her.

He loved her. He'd admitted it. He loved her, yet he'd pushed her away. For days she'd struggled to soothe her bruised pride, believing he'd dumped her. She'd told herself that she didn't need him. Survival instincts had kicked in. She'd labored to accept that she couldn't make him love her. She'd wrestled with self-pity. Over and over she'd told herself that she'd lived without him before, she could again.

According to Rachel, none of what had happened was because of her. Max had just confirmed it was because of him. Did he truly believe he was the devil incarnate, a danger to anyone who got close to him? Was that really why he'd kept his distance from love?

In the kitchen, Sam turned on the faucet and filled a glass. Now what? If he loved her, everything she longed for could be theirs. Her stomach queasy, she took several deep breaths before raising the glass to her lips. Shifting her stance, she leaned against the counter. That's when she saw him.

He stood so still, looked so lonely. Her heart thudding, she vowed not to fall apart in front of him. She needed to be tough, steel her feelings. Though he'd made that admittance about love, that didn't mean she would hear the same words or that anything had changed.

"Do you mind if I turn that off?" he asked, indicating the radio and the music blaring from it.

"Go ahead." Never had she played the sweet, I'm-so-glad-to-see-you female. Even if she'd felt that way. She was used to giving what she got, and he'd given her a good case of heartache. All her life, she'd battled adversities to get what she wanted, had never backed down. And in one instant, with him closer now than he'd been in days, she had but one thought: she wanted to rush into his arms.

"I'm glad you're the one taking care of Rachel," he said.

Why did he come to her? "Rachel's become a friend." Sam waited while he switched off the music. "But what she needs most right now is family."

"I couldn't stay away."

That admittance said so much to Sam. The Max he'd been wouldn't have felt that way. He'd have kept even his sister at arm's length. So maybe he hadn't completely lapsed into his old ways. Maybe that gentler Max still was around.

"Sam—"

Her eyes whipped to him. She couldn't play word games with him. She was hurting. That was his fault. "You think I'll be better off without you," she said.

Max felt as if she was reading his mind. How could he make her understand? Maybe he couldn't. No sparkle, no smile lit up her eyes. Questions filled them. And hurt. He shouldn't have listened to Rachel who'd urged him to talk to Sam. It was a mistake to seek her out. He couldn't even say why he'd followed her. He knew they didn't belong together.

"Max, answer me," she demanded. "Is that why this happened?"

It happened because I love you. He cursed himself for the emotion. "It's best," he finally answered.

"I don't believe that. Did you lie to Rachel?" As if preparing for a punch, her chin raised a notch. "Or do you love me?"

How could he not love her? She was warm, sensitive, beautiful, accepting. There was the biggie. She would accept him despite all his faults. "Yes, I love you," he answered because he couldn't lie to her.

He saw hope flicker in her eyes and damned himself for arousing it in her.

"Then this makes no sense, Max."

Because it was too painful to meet her stare, he looked away, took a step from her.

In a defiant move, she blocked his path. "Max, talk to me."

Eyes filled with hurt pinned him. "There's nothing to say." Max strode to a window. On a chaise longue, Jack balanced Alyssa on his bent knees and bounced her. He had it all, didn't he? A loving wife, a family. They were what mattered most. Max had known that, but couldn't reach out for all he wanted, couldn't hurt the woman he loved. "I hurt Michelle. I wasn't there for Christina. How many chances do I get to screw up people's lives?"

"What happened with Michelle was an accident.

That's why it's called an accident. The only one who's miserable is you," Sam argued.

She was wrong. "I was responsible for what happened to her." For so long since he'd awakened with amnesia, he'd agonized to remember his past. Now that he had, he longed to forget what had happened.

"According to Rachel, Michelle has gone on with her life. She's married, and has a little boy, doesn't she?"

"What does that—"

Her eyes danced but not with a smile. Fire flared in them. "You're the one who's stuck in the past."

"I'm the one who nearly killed her."

Even if they didn't find their way to each other, Sam wanted peace of mind for him. "Max, you had an accident."

"I shouldn't have been driving."

"Okay, maybe you shouldn't have, although from what I've been told I think you're too hard on yourself. Rachel said the police didn't fault you. The weather was terrible that day. The accident could have happened to anyone. And how can you blame yourself for what happened to your sister?"

"She wanted me that day, Sam." He stood ramrod-straight, so tense he looked as if he'd break. "I should have gone to her."

"Would that have changed the outcome?"

"Who knows."

"Yes. Who knows. So why do you believe that if you

went to her that day, she'd still be alive? You don't know that, do you? Why do you want the past to over-shadow all you could have now? Why are you blaming yourself for something you had no control over?"

"Sam, I'm not going to hurt you."

She was sure he'd moved a step closer, almost reached out for her. Then, as if catching himself, he took a step to the side, putting the table between them. "You are hurting me," she said softly. What would it take to make him hear her words instead of the ones in his mind?

"You're not protecting me from anything. You're hurting me by pushing me away. And why? Because of guilt you don't deserve." Her voice broke. Sam hated that, detested women who used tears, but she barely kept a handle on them.

"You don't understand."

"But I do." She blinked against the burning at the backs of her eyes. "I'm a nurse. Anyone in medicine has moments when they wish they could do more. When they lose a patient, they feel such helplessness. They—" She stopped, her voice trailing off. All that was wrong seemed so obvious suddenly. "Oh, Max." His pain weaved its way through her. She swayed back against the counter. How could she help him? As her throat tightened, she heaved a breath. All she wanted to do was to cry for him. She'd been trying to compre-hend why he'd gathered the blame and guilt to him like treasures. Now she knew. "Not getting too close to anyone is safer, isn't it?"

His gaze sliced to her. "What did you say?"

"That's why you stayed clear of your sisters, didn't get involved in their lives. This isn't about protecting them or me. It's about protecting yourself."

He stared at her eyes, dark and moist with hurt. "You're making no sense." He shook his head, turned away. "There's no point in talking about this anymore."

"You're so stubborn."

He heard her tears, but kept his back to her. Too many thoughts, too many emotions bombarded him. With a half turn, he inhaled a hard breath and watched her walk out of the room. She'd said he was hurting her. Hurting her by pushing her away.

Through the back door window, he saw her standing on the patio, watching Jack and Alyssa. He could have what Jack had. He could be with Sam. Longing. Desire. Love. They were such a part of him—because of her.

Almost entranced by the scene in front of him, he watched Alyssa. On blind faith that Jack would catch her, she charged forward on wobbly legs and threw herself into his arms. An innocent, she'd taken the chance with no fear. All that had mattered was being in her daddy's arms.

Max sucked in a breath. The little one had courage, far more than he. Sam had been right. This was about him.

He didn't remember consciously opening the door, but he was staring at her slender back. Aching. *Sam.* He didn't think he'd said her name out loud. But she turned, faced him, as if sensing him there. What words would lessen the hurt he'd caused her? "We need to talk," he insisted.

"Do we?"

Under his breath he swore at his own ineptness. He took a deep breath as a calming measure. Instead he took in her scent, and could barely think straight again. "You were right," he blurted.

"I was right?"

He saw again the hope in her eyes, and it gave him some of his own. "I've been mixed up, I guess."

Sam couldn't talk. A lump settled in her throat. Tears smarted the backs of her eyes. Even as she craved to feel his arms around her, she kept her feet rooted to the spot. But she was hopeful. There was a softness in his gaze she'd been yearning to see.

"Getting close to anyone is risky."

"Is that what this is about, Max? Are you afraid of losing someone you love?"

"It happened before." He avoided her eyes, the concern in them. "Losing Michelle had hurt. I loved her deeply, Sam," he admitted. "When she nearly died, I felt such guilt." The pain of that moment in his life seemed a breath away suddenly. "Then she turned away from me. Well, why wouldn't she? I had hurt her. I nearly destroyed her life, killed her."

"Oh, Max."

He made himself meet her stare. "I can't explain what happened then. I just knew I never wanted to feel that again."

So he locked out loved ones, Sam mused. "Max, we

don't get guarantees that if we love, then we'll never lose."

"Yeah, I know. And I want one." That was what he wanted most. A guarantee. A guarantee that he could love Sam and not lose her. He knew he wasn't free of the guilt or his fear. He couldn't switch off feelings with a blink of the eye, and he still believed caring and loving was risky. He heard Alyssa's giggle and looked away. But like her, with blind faith, he had to take a risk. "I love you, Sam, and it scares the hell out of me. But I know now that I'll die inside without you."

In a move more tender than she'd ever recalled, his hand framed her face. She couldn't stand it another minute. Happiness at hearing those words bubbled within her. She didn't need him to beg. She closed the few inches between them. She touched his chest, then slid her hand upward and curled it around his neck.

"I know that I—" he started.

"Messed up?"

For the first time since that night when he'd turned away from her, Max felt like smiling. Gently he brushed her hair away from her face. He'd been taken with her feisty ways from the first moment he'd met her. "What I want…what I need most, is you. I don't want to live my life without you." A tenseness entered his eyes. "Hell, I'm not easy. I know that. But I hope you still want me."

Sam's heart swelled that he was trying so hard. "Sometimes I'm not easy, either," she said, aware she didn't always keep her mouth shut when she should.

"Yeah, you're really hard to take." His arm tightened at her waist, and he buried his face in her hair.

"I know I can be—"

"Wonderful," he murmured. "Caring."

His words thrilled her. *You were right, Mama. There was a Mr. Right for me.* Tenderly she caressed his jaw. "Anything else?" she asked on a laugh, wanting to do something to take the agony from his eyes.

"All of the above and more." Slowly a smile spread across his face. "I love you, Sam," he said quietly. "I want to marry you."

Elation coursed through her. Dreams of a lifetime were within her grasp. This was a beginning. This was all she'd been wanting. "Max, I love you, too."

He answered her with a husky laugh and closed his mouth over hers. In his kiss was a message of deep love, a promise of always. You're necessary to me. You're a part of me, his kiss said.

Even as Max hungered, he fought the desire to crush her to him. He took in the sight of her smile, of those laughing green eyes. "To think I'd nearly lost you," he said raggedly as the realization moved through him. Against him, he felt her tremble with a sigh. "Sam, I'll love you forever, give you anything you want."

Though her expression remained deadly serious, her eyes sparkled with a tease. "Breakfast in bed?"

Almost reverently he brushed a single strand of hair back from her cheek. "And a garden. A horse. Anything."

Sam let the moment filled with love seep over her.

There was one part of her dream she'd always kept harbored deep within, afraid to believe it would come true. "There is something else," she admitted.

Max had meant what he'd said. He'd give her anything she wanted. "Name it."

Sam knew the risk she would be asking him to take. But a lifetime of happiness for her and him was a yes away. "How do you feel about babies?" she asked.

A child. In an instant, without any warning, a tinge of fear galloped through Max. A child—their child—would be someone else to love. He grabbed a quick breath.

And someone who'd love back, the small voice in his head reminded him. Wasn't this the ultimate dragon to confront? Face it, he railed at himself. He couldn't go through life afraid to love. He had to take risks to have this woman—and a family with her. "I never thought I'd say this. But there's nothing I want more."

Through a mist of tears, Sam smiled up at him. "You're a changed man, Max Montgomery," she said on a soft laugh. Joy warming her, she kissed him long and hard.

"Because of you," Max murmured against her lips. "Because of you."

* * * * *

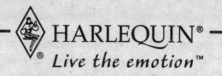

HARLEQUIN®
Live the emotion™

Love, Home & Happiness

HARLEQUIN® *Blaze*

Red-hot reads.

HHH Harlequin® Historical
Historical Romantic Adventure!

HARLEQUIN® *Romance*
From the Heart, For the Heart

Breathtaking Romantic Suspense

Medical Romance™...
love is just a heartbeat away

Seduction and Passion Guaranteed!

HARLEQUIN® *Super Romance*®
Exciting, Emotional, Unexpected

www.eHarlequin.com

HDIRC

HARLEQUIN® *Romance*®

The rush of falling in love

Cosmopolitan
international settings

Believable, feel-good stories
about today's women

The compelling thrill
of romantic excitement

It could happen to you!

EXPERIENCE
HARLEQUIN ROMANCE!

Available wherever Harlequin books are sold.

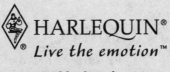

HARLEQUIN®
Live the emotion™

www.eHarlequin.com

HROMDIR09

HARLEQUIN®

Invites *you* to experience lively, heartwarming all-American romances

Every month, we bring you four strong, sexy men, and four women who know what they want—and go all out to get it.

From small towns to big cities, experience a sense of adventure, romance and family spirit—the all-American way!

Love, Home & Happiness

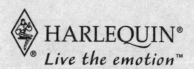
HARLEQUIN®
Live the emotion™

www.eHarlequin.com   HARDIR08

HARLEQUIN®
INTRIGUE®

BREATHTAKING ROMANTIC SUSPENSE

Shared dangers and passions lead to electrifying
romance and heart-stopping suspense!

Every month, you'll meet six new heroes
who are guaranteed to make your spine tingle
and your pulse pound. With them you'll enter
into the exciting world of Harlequin Intrigue—
where your life is on the line
and so is your heart!

THAT'S INTRIGUE—
ROMANTIC SUSPENSE
AT ITS BEST!

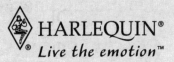

HARLEQUIN®
Live the emotion™

www.eHarlequin.com   INTDIR06

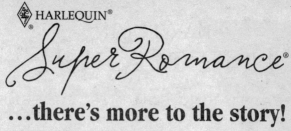

...there's more to the story!

Superromance.
A *big* satisfying read about unforgettable
characters. Each month we offer *six* very different
stories that range from family drama to adventure
and mystery, from highly emotional stories to
romantic comedies—and much more! Stories
about people you'll believe in and care about.
Stories too compelling to put down....

Our authors are among today's *best* romance
writers. You'll find familiar names and talented
newcomers. Many of them are award winners—
and you'll see why!

If you want the biggest and best
in romance fiction, you'll get it
from Superromance!

Exciting, Emotional, Unexpected...

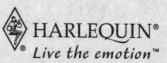

www.eHarlequin.com   HSDIR06

V ™ *Silhouette®*

SPECIAL EDITION™

Emotional, compelling stories that capture the intensity of living, loving and creating a family in today's world.

Special Edition features bestselling authors such as Susan Mallery, Sherryl Woods, Christine Rimmer, Joan Elliott Pickart— and many more!

For a romantic, complex and emotional read, choose Silhouette Special Edition.

Visit Silhouette Books at www.eHarlequin.com   SSEGEN06

SPECIAL EDITION™

Emotional, compelling stories that capture the intensity of living, loving and creating a family in today's world.

Modern, passionate reads that are powerful and provocative.

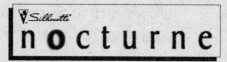

Dramatic and sensual tales of paranormal romance.

Romances that are sparked by danger and fueled by passion.